Praise for

MW00930000

"Cassie Premo Steele has written a stunner of a novel, one that speaks profoundly to (and of) our times, yet also carries a timeless wisdom — a wisdom that knows the power of art, the power of story, the power of love, yet also knows sometimes there are no easy answers. *The ReSisters* left me breathless and shaken and grateful."

~Gayle Brandeis, Author of *The Book of Dead Birds*, winner of the Bellwether Prize for Fiction of Social Engagement

"Weaving alternate history with ancient history, *The ReSisters* forms a herstory that transcends time and shines a light on the shadows with which America currently wrestles. Both timely and timeless, the story will leave you questioning your version of the American Dream and the impact of your own choices within it."

~Laraine Herring, author of *Writing Begins with the Breath*

"A suspenseful novel that reflects contemporary American realities. With a cast of intersectional feminist characters, including lesbian and transgender characters, the book inspires readers to ask critical questions about what constitutes the right action in the face of injustice. How do we hold our pain as we work toward healing? As 15-year-old narrator, Sanna, says, 'There's somehow some kind of wholeness that can be recovered in the world when women work together.'"

~Emily Withnall, contributor to *The Kenyon Review*

"After reading *The ReSisters*, I am still catching my breath. The book is haunting, harrowing, a statement. A warning, a blessing, a multi-faceted diamond enlightening us all."

~Barbara Straus Lodge, Founder of TruthTalks and Co-Editor of *Janeland*, a 2018 Lambda Literary Award Nominee

"*The ReSisters* offers a striking portrayal of a world that is both alarmingly possible and already here--a vision of a United States in which patriotism, nationalism, and xenophobia are valued above all else, and in which those who resist are targeted, detained, and endangered. At the same time, Steele offers us a glimmer of hope, revealing the many ways in which resistance can take root, heal, and grow. A chilling, moving, and all-too-possible story."

~Alexis Stratton, author of the
BLOOM chapbook "Fratricide"
and the blog *you are (queer) here*

"I read *The ReSisters* in one fascinated sitting, completely drawn into the story of a dystopian future already present in too many ways. Steele writes with a confident energy that is captivating—I could not put down the novel until I learned the fate of Sanna, an indigenous teenage girl whose life has been blown apart. She won my heart."

~Susan Power, Author of *Sacred Wilderness* and *The Grass Dancer*, Winner of the Ernest Hemingway Foundation Award for First Fiction

The ReSisters

for Phoebe—

A novel by

Cassie Premo Steele
with art by Amy Alley

healer like Eden, mother like Parker ♡

Cassie Premo Steele

October 20, 2018

*Phoebe—
Keep being a
ReSister! ♡*

Amy Alley

ISBN: 978-1-7327237-1-9

Library of Congress Control Number: 2018956984

Illustrations and cover art by Amy Alley

Back cover by Susanne Kappler

For Lily and Eric and the seven generations.

Part One

1.

Sanna sees the news filling up her Twitter feed and decides to text her mom.

Sanna: Mom? You okay?
Tembe: Yes. Just landed.
Sanna: Have you seen the news?
Tembe: No. What happened?
Sanna: Another terror attack.
Tembe: Where?
Sanna: New York.
Tembe: But where?
Sanna: Near the Brooklyn Bridge.
Tembe: Everything is fine here.
Sanna: Ok.
Tembe: Don't worry. I have to go through Customs now. They don't allow cell phones in line. I'll text you when I get through.
Sanna: Ok. Love you!
Tembe: Love you, Chickadee.

2.

The news is scrolling on the televisions while Tembe waits in line at JFK. She's tired. Up early for a flight from Amsterdam, and it's only three-thirty in the afternoon in New York but it feels like bedtime. After Customs, she has one more flight to Raleigh, and then she will be home in time for Halloween. Her daughter Sanna loves dressing as Spearfinger. Even though the other kids don't know who she is supposed to be, the pointy finger glove that Tembe made for Sanna to wear scares them as she hands out the candy.

Tembe looks at the two lines in front of her, labeled Citizen and Non-Citizen, and heads toward the one for citizens, sending quiet prayers to those in the other line, given what's been happening in the past two years. Despite everything, she is glad she can get in this line.

A text comes in from Parker, and Tembe can see the notification light up in her open bag, but Tembe is at the front of the line now. She'll respond later.

She hands her passport to the pale, chubby Customs agent behind the counter.

"Business or pleasure?" he asks, not looking up.

"Business," she says, and he looks up at her, his arrival stamp hovering over the ghoulish green paper.

"What kind of business?"

"Art. I'm an artist. I had a show at the Hague."

He doesn't respond.

"The Hague. In the Netherlands." She is almost used to this, the way her long dark hair and deep brown eyes elicit suspicion in airports.

Almost. It's been bad for a long time, but in the past couple years, it is worse than ever.

"What kind of artist?" His eyes narrow.

"Mixed media," she says, but realizes this is too vague, and adds, "Painting. Collage. Based on Native American history."

He raises one eyebrow, glances down at the passport, and puts the arrival stamper down.

"Native American?"

"Yes," she says, tired of this. Bone tired. Weary.

"But your passport is from the United States."

"Yes," she says, a tinge of anger in her voice. "I'm a citizen."

"But you're Native American?"

"Cherokee."

He draws in a big breath and lets it out slowly.

"An enrolled member of the tribe?"

"Yes."

"I see. Wait one moment."

He leaves his perch behind the counter and goes to a tall man, says something, and they both look at her. Then they walk toward her.

Her heart skips a beat. She can see they mean harm.

"Ma'am," says the tall man. "Please come with me."

"Why?"

His blue eyes flash at the question but he says nothing, opens the waist-high swinging door between them, and waits for her to walk through.

She hesitates for less than a second. In that second is her love for her daughter, for her family, for her life.

And then she walks through.

She is led down a white hallway through the bowels of the airport. She will miss her connecting flight to Raleigh if this takes more than an hour. But she suspects this should not be her greatest concern right now.

In a small room, there is a man sitting at a table with a video recorder propped up in the corner on a small tripod.

"Tembe Penbrook," says the tall man and hands her passport to the man in a beige suit who does not stand for her.

"Have a seat," the sitting beige man says. "I am Detective Burney with HSI. I just have a few questions."

"HSI?" she says, pulling out the metal chair.

"Homeland Security Investigations. The investigative arm of DHS."

As she sits, he turns on the video recorder.

"Please state your full name."

"Tembe Penbrook."

"That's it?" he asks.

For a second, she thinks this is a case of mistaken identity. Maybe he was expecting someone else. But the tall man said her name.

"No middle name?" he asks.

She closes her eyes, just briefly, considering her options. The middle name is not on the passport. But if she lies to authorities, that would be a crime. And they would have grounds to arrest her. So she opens her eyes and says it.

"Warmaker."

"War maker?" he asks.

"My middle name. Warmaker."

His lips go up so slightly that she thinks of Mona Lisa. "Well, Ms. Tembe Warmaker Penbrook, do you know why you've been detained for questioning?"

"I have no idea."

"How long have you been out of the country?"

"Two weeks," she says, and remembers the way the October leaves were just beginning to turn red on the dogwood in the front yard the morning she left.

"I see," he says. "Well, maybe you didn't get to hear the news, but the ONE policy was passed while you were away."

"One?"

"One Nation Education," he says. "Everyone with dual citizenship will be enrolled in a program of patriotic allegiance."

"Dual citizenship?"

"You are Cherokee, right?"

She nods. She is a member of the Cherokee Nation. "I didn't realize that was considered a crime."

"It's not a crime," he says. "It's a policy."

"Policy?"

"Yes, ma'am. Let me explain what's going to happen. You can make one phone call to let someone know what's happening, and then you will be transported to a ONE facility."

"Where?"

"I'm not at liberty to say."

"Not at liberty," Tembe repeats, and now it's her turn to let her lips do the Mona Lisa.

"That's right. Now, do you have your cell phone?"

"Yes," she says and thinks of the text from Parker. "But do I get a lawyer?"

"No, ma'am. The government is not obligated to provide lawyers in civil cases concerning immigration and citizenship. And anyway, this is not a legal case. It is a policy instituted and overseen jointly by the Departments of Justice and Homeland Security."

"So I can use my phone call to contact a lawyer if I pay for one on my own?"

"Your choice. Most people call a family member, though. We used to confiscate the phones and make people use our landlines, but hardly anyone knows numbers anymore. After that, we will take your phone."

"Take my phone? Isn't that illegal search and seizure?"

"As I said, ma'am, this is not a legal matter. It's a policy. I'll leave you alone while you make your call, but the video camera will keep recording. We've seen that these calls can be emotional, so we want to give you as much privacy as possible."

"Privacy," she says, and there is an edge to her voice.

"You've got two minutes," Detective Burney says and stands up to leave the room.

Tembe looks at the camera. Pulls out her cell phone. Sees the unanswered text from Parker, her wife. And a new text from Sanna, her daughter. She could call either one of them. She should call either one of them. Who wouldn't call their family at a time like this? Although Tembe doesn't use her middle name, saying it out loud just now has brought it into the room. She didn't make this war, but she's in it now. And she's a Warmaker.

3.

"Sanna, have you heard from your mom?" Parker asks as Sanna comes out of her room in the Spearfinger costume.

She's wearing a long gray robe and a wig with long gray hair, and it could be any kind of scary character, except for the glove that holds a long finger with a spear at the tip.

It's nowhere near sunset, but Sanna loves the Cherokee story of Spearfinger that her mother has told her since she was a little girl, and this is the one time of year when she can wear the costume. She knows she's too old, at fifteen, for trick or treating, but she likes to give out candy and cackle in the evil granny voice at the children.

"A while ago," says Sanna. "She'd just landed and was going through Customs."

"What time was that?" Parker asks, looking at her phone.

"Three-thirty maybe? Maybe Customs took longer than she expected? And she had to rush to her next flight?" Sanna suggests. Parker's a worrier, so Sanna pretends not to be worried. "I'm sure she's fine," she says. "Where's the Halloween candy?"

"In the garage," Parker says. "I didn't want us to eat it so I put it away." She brushes her chin-length light brown hair behind her ear as she grins at Sanna. Parker's always a bit chubby and says life is too sweet not to eat sweets.

Sanna smiles at her. Her stepmother is cautious like that, a planner like that. She has come to appreciate it, although at first it seemed uptight. When Parker first met Sanna, she couldn't really see what her mother liked about her. It's been ten years, though, and the word "stepmother" doesn't really even apply anymore. She's a mom.

Sanna goes to the garage and maneuvers around the bikes and lawn equipment to get to the food shelf. There are canned goods and nonperishables here that Parker has stocked up on. Just in case.

There aren't many emergencies in North Carolina, but they did have a hurricane once that made it to the middle of the state with winds and flooding, and the family was glad Parker had her stash when it happened. Sanna smiles again to see the soups and beans and vegetables lined up neatly in cans on the shelves, grabs the three bags of candy, and heads back into the house.

"Sanna," Parker says, almost running into her in the kitchen. "Can you text your mom for me?"

"I did a while ago."

"I know. But can you text her again?" Parker's face is paler than usual, her forehead more creased in worry.

"Okay," says Sanna, and sends her mom a heart emoji.

The text does not say "Read" or even "Delivered."

"It's not going through," says Sanna.

"Neither are any of mine," says Parker. "It's after four-thirty. If she made it through Customs, she'll be on the flight to Raleigh by now. But I can't believe she wouldn't text us."

4.

Tembe scrolls through her contacts to S and clicks on the name of Hadassah Seigel. The detective was right; she wouldn't have been able to remember Hadassah's number. She can't believe it, but even now, she is capable of feeling grateful.

Hadassah picks up right away. For this, too, Tembe is grateful.

"Tembe?" Hadassah answers. "Are you okay?"

Tembe can hear the news on in the background. Hadassah always has the news on whenever she's home. She feels it's her responsibility to stay informed, however fruitless that may be. Tembe likes that about her.

"Yes," Tembe says, knowing that Hadassah, like Sanna and the rest of the nation, is riveted by the latest terror attack. "Listen," she says. "I need you to turn the television down."

There is a pause. Then silence. Then Hadassah says, "What is it?"

"I have been detained as part of the ONE policy," Tembe says. "And I am being video recorded right now."

"I understand."

Tembe knows that Hadassah has been preparing for a moment like this all her life. Maybe before her life even began. Maybe even back to her parents' lives in Germany, and later, in Israel. This history, this shared story despite their differences, this is why Tembe decided to call her. Despite the knives of love and loyalty that are cutting into her belly even now as she tries not to think about Sanna and Parker and how they'll react when they discover that this was the one phone call she decided to make. Despite the nausea rising even now in her throat as she pushes away her desire to hear their loving voices at this very moment.

"Protect it," Tembe says, her voice not even a whisper, almost a ghost of a sound in the empty room with the video recorder flashing red at her.

"I will," Hadassah says. Her voice is strong. It gives Tembe a sliver of strength, enough to be able to say their names out loud.

"Tell Sanna and Parker that I love them," she says, her voice shaking as the HSI detective opens the door.

"I will," Hadassah says again.

Tembe hangs up and quickly deletes the record of the call in her phone. She doubts it will make any difference, but she does it just in case.

And the detective holds out his hand for her phone. His eyes are blue like ice.

5.

The first kids to come for trick or treating are always the youngest, those who have an early bedtime and might be afraid of the dark anyway.

Their parents come up on the porch, sometimes with children in their arms, little pumpkins and ghosts and ninjas and princesses.

Sanna decides to save her scary stuff for later, uses her regular voice to say "Happy Halloween!" and smiles as she drops the candy in the bags.

After they leave, she shuts the door and turns around to see Parker looking white as a ghost.

"What's wrong?" Sanna says.

Parker says nothing, stands with her arms crossed over herself, and something about this gesture makes Nick, Parker's son, look up from his laptop on the couch and take his earbuds out.

"Mom?" Nick says. "What is it?"

"Sit down with me," she says, and Nick pulls up his long, seventeen-year-old legs and sits like a regular person on the couch so Parker can sit next to him. Sanna sits next to Parker.

"It's your mom," Parker says. She is speaking mostly to Sanna, although her mom is also legally Nick's mom, too.

Sanna says nothing. She looks down at the long, pointed finger on the glove her mom made her. Her stomach hurts. Her stomach always hurts when she's worried. She feels like one of the little kids that Spearfinger captured. She takes off the glove and balls it into her fist.

"What," she says, not able to make her voice inflect into a question, just wanting the answer, wanting this moment to be over.

"She's been detained at the airport. I just got a call," Parker says.

"What?" Nick finally closes his laptop.

"There's a new policy," Parker explains. "I heard about it but didn't think anything about it. I didn't think Tembe would qualify. It didn't occur to me."

Sanna is silent.

"What new policy?" Nick asks.

"It's called ONE. One Nation Education. It was signed last week, but I didn't think it would go into effect right away. I thought there would be an injunction."

"Crap," Nick says. Sanna knows he's a news junkie. She knows he knows what Parker is talking about. But she only wants to know one thing. She doesn't care about politics or policies or injunctions.

"Parker," Sanna says, her voice cracking, "where's my mom?"

6.

Tembe has nothing. They have taken her phone, her ID, her purse and carry-on bag. She checked her baggage and she doesn't know if it went onto the flight to Raleigh or is still somewhere at JFK.

Tembe has nothing. She didn't get to hear Sanna or Parker's voices since she decided to call Hadassah instead of calling them, so she doesn't even have the memory of that conversation.

Tembe has nothing. She doesn't have her hands because they have handcuffed them behind her back. She asked why this was necessary, but she wasn't given an answer, so she doesn't have that.

And then she remembers something Hadassah told her once. The guards in the concentration camp, Hadassah's parents had told her, had a saying that they used frequently: "Hier ist kein warum."

Here there is no why.

They said it when prisoners asked why there were there. They said it when prisoners asked why this was happening. Why they had to dig a ditch. Why someone was shot.

And Tembe remembers, in that way that memory sometimes works, that it was this story about the absence of sense, the lack of reason, the terrible turn toward meaninglessness, that put in motion her phone call to Hadassah.

It was ostensibly the book that Tembe was trying to protect with the phone call. The book, a new art work that Tembe finished right before her trip to The Hague, that Tembe left in her office at the college, that Hadassah would pick up that night, Tembe knew, and put somewhere safe. To protect Tembe. To protect her family.

But it wasn't just the book.

It was the fact that if she'd called Parker or Tembe, she would have heard the one word that would make her answer, no matter what she said, in an echo of the guards at the camp.

"Why?"

Tembe called Hadassah, not only to save her art, but also so she wouldn't have to hear this question come from the mouths of the people she loved most in the world.

Because in answer to this question, Tembe has nothing.

7.

Sanna is angry. She's making Parker repeat the story again. Even though Parker is crying, and even though saying the words is painful to her. Parker is not her mother, and her mother is not here, and Sanna is angry about that, too.

"Say it again."

"Sanna," Parker pleads, "I don't know any more than you do. I've told you all I know."

"Say it again."

Parker looks at her and wipes the tears from her cheeks. Takes a deep breath. Sanna knows that Parker would rather see Sanna sad than angry. Parker would rather have a daughter who was more like her. But she's not. She's not like her. She's not her daughter. She's Tembe's daughter, and she's angry.

"Okay," Parker says. "Hadassah called me and told me that your mom called her. I don't know why she called her and not us." Her voice wobbles as she says this, and then she widens her eyes. "Maybe she wanted to stay strong. Maybe it was too hard to call us," she says.

"But tell me again *why*."

"It's because your mom is," Parker starts to say, and then pauses. "It's because your mom is not considered a *pure citizen* according to the new ONE policy. Because she's also a member of the Cherokee Nation."

"But I'm not?"

"No," Parker says. "Your mom didn't enroll you. Your dad ...."

Sanna doesn't want to think about her dad, and she is furious that this has to come up right now. That has nothing to do with this.

"Yeah, okay," she says. "Whatever. She didn't enroll me because she didn't want to contact my dad. Okay. So that means I'm a pure citizen because I'm a bastard? How fucked up is that logic?"

"Sanna," Parker says, about to admonish her for swearing, but shakes her head. "I'm sorry, honey. I don't know anything else. I'll start making phone calls first thing in the morning. You can stay home with me tomorrow. You don't have to go to school."

"What about me?" Nick says.

"You can stay home, too. You can both stay home tomorrow."

Sanna knows that Parker is always trying to treat them equally. But they're not equal. He is her blood. Sanna is not.

The doorbell rings.

"Trick or treat!"

Sanna opens her fist to the crumpled Spearfinger glove she's been holding, and then puts it back on. She stands up from the couch and gets the bowl of candy and opens the door.

Her evil granny cackle is louder and more terrifying than ever.

The kids scream.

Maybe this is sick, but it actually makes Sanna feel a little bit better to scare them and hear them scream.

That way, she is not the only child who is frightened tonight.

8.

After the last trick or treater is treated to Spearfinger's terror, Sanna blows out the candles in the pumpkins on the front porch and turns out the light.

Parker has already gone to bed. As it was, she stayed up past her bedtime. Sleep, Sanna knows, is Parker's drug of choice, helped along by a glass or two of red wine after dinner.

Sanna suddenly realizes that they didn't have dinner. Parker is an excellent cook and loves the process of it, the menu making and the shopping and the cooking and, most especially, the "eating together as a family" that they do.

But not tonight.

Parker forgot to cook dinner. Nick and Sanna forgot to be hungry. And Tembe forgot to come home.

Sanna knows that's not what happened. But she doesn't really know what happened, not really, so she tells herself it was a kind of forgetting.

"Hey, Squirta," Nick says, from the couch, where he's been all night as Sanna handed out the candy. This is his nickname for her, ever since they met, when Sanna was five and he was seven and already tall and lanky. "Wanna see something?"

Sanna doesn't say anything but goes to sit by Nick. She's not tired. She's not hungry. She's not feeling anything really, so it doesn't matter to her what he wants her to see, maybe a funny GIF to cheer her or some video of a Halloween prank.

It's not.

It's her mom.

"What is this?" Sanna asks.

"It's an underground network," Nick says. "I started doing some digging around after my mom went to bed. I was Googling ONE and found a thread on Twitter where some dude said he had photos from the New York education center, so I stalked him a little bit and found he's a member of 8space, which you have to sign up for, so I did."

Sanna can't quite wrap her head around all this, but there it is, in grainy color: a photo of her mom, handcuffed, walking down a hallway.

"Where is this?"

"I told you. The education center in New York. I thought you'd be happy."

"Happy?" Sometimes Sanna does not understand Nick at all.

"To see her, I mean," Nick says. His face gets that little pout it always does when he's disappointed.

"To see that she's not dead, you mean?" Sanna's voice lifts a little, and they both look down the hallway to where Parker is sleeping.

"No, man. That's not what I meant. I wanted to help."

The problem is that seeing this is making it more real for Sanna, and she was going to pretend that her mom's plane was late, or that she'd forgotten to come home, or even that she was already home and just sleeping. There are tears in Sanna's eyes.

"Squirta, I'm sorry."

"Thanks," she says. "I just don't know about this guy. Why did he take a picture of my mom and post it on the internet?"

"It wasn't just your mom. There are pictures of everyone who gets sent to the education center."

"You know what I mean. And why do you keep calling it that? My mom doesn't need more education. She has a graduate degree, just like your mom."

"I know. It's what they call it, though."

"It's a jail, Nick," Sanna says. "My mom is in jail. And there's no reason for it."

And just then Sanna has an idea. She looks at her phone. It's too late to call now. But she needs to talk to Dr. Seigel.

9.

When Sanna wakes, it is almost noon and she's starving. She checks her phone, as she does every morning, and there are Instagram and Twitter alerts but nothing pressing. Her last text to her mom is still undelivered. She thinks about writing another one but can't stand to see that one go unanswered, too, so she throws off the covers and shuffles into the kitchen.

"Hello, sleepyhead," says Parker at the breakfast table, holding coffee. It looks like she hasn't been up long, either. She's still in her nightgown. "I thought I'd let everyone sleep in today. Nick's still asleep."

"Yeah," Sanna says. "I sure wouldn't have been able to handle school today."

"That's what I thought," says Parker. "How are you doing?"

Sanna knows she means it, really wants to know how she's doing, but the cereal is just now hitting the bowl and Sanna hasn't had a bite, so she says, "Fine," and sits down at the table with Parker.

Parker lets her chew and swallow a few times as Sanna scrolls through her phone. Photos from Halloween parties with older kids at her school come up. The girls are mostly bunnies. The boys are mostly superheroes.

That gives her an idea. An idea that might get her closer to her plan from last night.

"Parker," she says, putting the phone down, "Have you ever thought about the fact that the word superhero becomes feminine when it's plural?"

"What do you mean?" Parker asks and there's a glimmer of light in her eyes. Sanna knows that Parker loves this. She's a poet, and she loves language play, and she especially loves anything that reveals the hidden feminism in the world, just waiting to be discovered, in words.

"I mean," Sanna says. "Superhero is spelled s-u-p-e-r-h-e-r-o. With an O, right?"

"Yeah?" Parker is eating this up, Sanna can tell.

"But superheroes. That's s-u-p-e-r-h-e-r-o-e-s. With an E. Feminine ending, see?"

"Yes!" Parker smiles. "When it's plural, it's collective. Which is feminine!"

Sanna grins and takes another bite of cereal.

"Hey, Parker, I've been thinking."

"Yeah?"

"I want to be a superheroe with an E."

"What do you mean?"

"I mean, I want to call Dr. Seigel and ask her about why my mom called her instead of us."

Parker stops smiling. "Absolutely not."

10.

"Absolutely not what?" Nick says, scratching his bushy blond hair as he sits down at the breakfast table.

Parker jumps up to pour him cereal, which gets on Sanna's last nerve. She's such a feminist except when it comes to her son. It's like the mother part of her overrides the feminist part of her when he's around.

"I want to call Hadassah. I want to know why mom called her instead of us," says Sanna.

Nick nods, but it's a slow nod. A thoughtful nod.

Parker places a bowl of cereal in front of him and sits back down at the table.

"It's not a good idea, Sanna," she says.

"Why not?" asks Nick, but Sanna can't really tell if he's on her side or just wanting to hear what his mom has to say so he can agree with her.

"Well," Parker says, and then takes a long, slow breath, "what's happening to your mom is very dangerous. I didn't know last night. I thought it would be over fairly quickly. But I called a lawyer this morning."

"Who?" Nick asks.

"Dixon. That friend of your father's."

Sanna sees Nick shudder a little as he says, "That guy's such a scum. I can't believe you called him."

"Nick," says Parker. "He's a good lawyer."

"Scum."

"Anyway," Parker says, focused directly on Sanna. "He said that we should not do anything out of the ordinary. No phone calls or visits to people we don't normally see. Your mom, if she goes along with the education program, can be out in six months."

"Six months?" Sanna almost yells.

"But if she doesn't cooperate, or if they have any reason to suspect that she's not loyal to the ONE program, if any of her family members aren't loyal, they can hold her on other charges."

"What other charges?" Sanna asks.

"APA," says Nick.

"What's that?" asks Sanna.

"Anti-patriotic attitude. I read about it last night on the 8space," he says.

"Nick, you know I don't like you going on those sites," says Parker.

"I know, Mom. I was trying to help."

"Wait," says Sanna. "You're telling me that my mom has to spend at least six months in this place, and maybe more, if she has, or they suspect that she has, or if we have, or if they suspect that we have an *attitude problem*?"

"Exactly," say Parker and Nick together.

"We're fucked."

11.

Later, when Parker is in the shower, Sanna goes to Parker's phone. It's locked. She tries a few combinations. Their wedding date. Nope. Her mother's birthday. Nope. Nick's birthday. Voilà!

She clicks on the Contacts button and scrolls to S. There it is. Hadassah Seigel.

Sanna wishes she could just text the contact info to herself, but she's afraid there would be a record of that, so she writes the number down on a piece of paper just as she hears Parker turning off the water in the bathroom.

She hurries to her room.

A while later, Parker knocks on her door. "Sanna, can I come in?"

"Sure."

Sanna's afraid Parker knows she's been on her phone, so she sits up and smiles. Acting innocent. She's seen it work when Nick does it.

"Honey, I want to talk to you. But," she says, lowering her voice, "not in the house. Will you go for a walk with me?"

Sanna can't believe it's already come to this, that Parker thinks their house might be bugged. But she just nods and says, "Give me a minute to get dressed."

When Parker is gone, she slips on a pair of jeans and a rust-colored sweatshirt, and then looks at the calendar on her wall, remembers it's November now and switches the page. The photo shows the leaves turning on the Blue Ridge Parkway near Cherokee, and the leaves in the mountains match her sweatshirt, as well as the dogwood in their front yard. The color of dried blood red.

Not expecting to see anyone from school at one in the afternoon in their neighborhood, she skips putting on makeup and pulls her long brown hair into a simple ponytail, and the word pony has her suddenly remembering something her mother told her.

"Horses aren't even indigenous," she'd said. "They came from Spain. The whole Indian on horseback thing. It's a product of colonialism."

Somehow it comforts Sanna to remember this small, fierce nugget of knowledge from her mom.

Parker is waiting by the front door. Nick's on his perch on the couch.

"We're going for a walk," Parker tells him.

Nick nods but doesn't even take his earbuds out.

Once they are away from the house, Parker says, "I want to talk to you about something and I didn't want Nick to hear."

Sanna laughs.

"Why are you laughing?" Parker looks concerned.

"I totally thought you thought the house was bugged!"

Parker smiles. "Am I that crazy?"

"Sometimes," Sanna says, and laughs again. It's true, Parker *is* sometimes that paranoid. Tembe called it cautious and caring, and Sanna thinks now that maybe her mom should have had more of this quality. Maybe now her mom wouldn't be where she is.

"No, I don't think the house is bugged," says Parker, "but I do think your mom is in a great deal of trouble. And I wanted to talk to you about it without Nick around. I don't want to fuel his conspiracy theory thinking."

"It's not really a theory any more, is it?" asks Sanna, thinking of the website he showed her the night before.

"Well, no. But we have to be realistic."

"Those 8space guys are as real as it gets."

"Maybe what I mean is pragmatic."

"Okay. Sorry. Go ahead." Sanna knows Parker wants her language to be precise. Like a knife. But it's harder for her to talk than to write.

"I know this is hard for you," Parker says. "It's hard for me, too. And in his own weird boy way, this is hard for Nick. But we have to go on as normal. We can't allow them to see anything we do as cause for suspicion. It might hurt your mom."

"You said all that at breakfast already," Sanna argues. "Why did you want to go on a walk to talk to me? Why didn't you want Nick to hear it?"

"Because Nick," Parker starts to say and then pauses. "Nick, you know, doesn't have a great relationship with his dad."

"Truth," says Sanna. Nick's dad is a senator and they rarely ever speak. Sanna doesn't know the whole story, which is weird because he's her stepbrother, but there's clearly some history there that nobody wants to talk about. Sanna has even asked her mom about it, but she wouldn't say anything.

"Well," continues Parker, "Nick is very concerned about the direction the nation is taking. I mean, we all are. But for Nick it's personal. He sees his dad as part of the problem. I know he spends time in those chat rooms. I don't like it. But, you know, he's seventeen. I can't monitor everything."

"Parker," Sanna interrupts, "what are you trying to say to me?"

"I'm saying that we don't want to give Nick any more fuel than what's already in his head. About how things are. I'm trying to protect him."

"You're trying to protect *him*?" Sanna says, incredulous.

"Yes. I'm his mom," Parker says, looking right at her.

"What about my mom? Aren't you trying to protect her?" Sanna's voice rises.

"Of course," Parker says, beginning to walk down the street again as if she's heading in some definite direction. "That's why I called the lawyer. Dixon is a very good lawyer and he knows how the administration works. And we can't do anything out of the ordinary. To protect your mom. And to protect Nick. That's why I don't want you to talk to Hadassah."

"I still don't understand what Hadassah has to do with all of this."

"That's exactly what I'm trying to say," says Parker. "You and Hadassah have never spoken before. She's a colleague of ours at the college. I know her. Your mom knows her. But there would be no reason for you to get in touch with her out of the blue. That would be unusual activity that could flag further investigation."

Sanna suddenly sees what Parker's getting at.

"You think Hadassah knows something that would potentially harm my mom?"

"I know she does."

Sanna is stunned. What does this mean? Was her mom actually doing something wrong? Could the nation hold her on APA charges for real?

"I can't tell you anything else," Parker says, in that serious voice she uses to read her poems. "I'm doing this to protect you."

"And Nick?"

"And Nick."

"And my mom?"

"Of course. I'm a mom. She's a mom. The reason she called Hadassah and not us is that she was doing what a mom does. Protects."

There's something about this that doesn't sit quite right with Sanna, but she doesn't say anything. Instead, she reworks her plan.

12.

By the time Sanna wakes the next morning, Parker is back to her regular routine, having woken long before dawn. The house still smells of the smoke of sage, which Parker lights before sitting in the dark with just a candle to write poetry until the rest of the family wakes. Parker is an early morning poet, and Tembe a late night artist, often staying at her studio on campus long after everyone else has gone to bed.

Sanna glances at her phone before getting out of her own bed. The Halloween terror attack has moved the president to decry all immigrants and impure citizens, and Congress is moving to authorize more funds for the ONE policy. There's nothing specific about how many people have been detained, and certainly nothing in the news about her mother. It is all reported in the passive voice as if no one is actually making these decisions. They're just being done.

Sanna sighs and throws off the covers, shuffles into her bunny slippers and heads toward the bathroom.

"Sanna, knock on your brother's door to make sure he's up, will you?" Parker calls from the kitchen. "I'm making eggs."

She knocks on Nick's door in the shave-and-a-haircut rhythm that is their ritual and once again wishes Parker weren't quite so perky first thing in the day. Nick opens his door and she can see that his laptop is already fired up. She wonders if he even slept at all. She wonders what else he has discovered from those chat rooms.

"Mom's making eggs," she says. He rolls his eyes but says nothing. They both find eggs icky but can't complain because they know Parker finds great joy in feeding them protein before school.

At the breakfast table, Sanna and Nick eat silently, the yellow scrambled eggs barely chewed as they swallow quickly and begin to contemplate their days.

Sanna is not going to school, but the others don't know this. She takes care not to dress differently than she normally would and leaves the house at the same time she always does.

Instead of heading to the bus stop with Nick, though, she tells him that her friend Jenny has just gotten her license and is giving her a ride and goes in the opposite direction.

And Sanna passes Jenny's house. Keeps walking.

They live in a small town, small enough that she could be seen by one of the faculty members at the college where Parker and Tembe teach, so she puts the hood up on her gray sweatshirt and keeps her head down until she gets to the coffee shop near campus. Just doing this makes her think of all the black kids shot wearing hoodies. Although she has always been sickened by these shootings, she gets the irony of it now. That the hood goes up because you want to be invisible. To keep yourself safe. She keeps her head down and walks quickly.

Once inside the coffee shop, she's hit with the warm air of the brew and the fresh muffins, and she takes the hood off because everyone is on their laptops or phones or tablets and wouldn't even look up to see her anyway. She takes her phone out and is about to dial Dr. Seigel's number when she stops and thinks better of it.

She approaches a female college student with long blonde hair whose phone, much larger than Sanna's, is sitting next to her laptop, which is open to a website showing twenty-five images of expensive boots. Some of those boots on the page cost more than her mothers pay for their mortgage each month.

"Excuse me," Sanna says in a sweet voice. "Can I borrow your phone for a sec? My battery is dead. I forgot to plug it in last night and I need to call a professor about an assignment."

"Sure," the girl says, barely looking at her, clicking on an image of black thigh-high boots. "Go ahead."

"Thanks." Sanna smiles, and takes the phone, steps a few feet away, and dials.

"Hello?" Dr. Seigel answers.

Sanna sighs a breath of relief since hardly anyone she knows answers their phone anymore if they don't recognize the number.

"Dr. Seigel?" Sanna says. "This is Sanna Penbrook."

"Sanna. Yes," Dr. Seigel says, as if she's been waiting for her to call.

"I—" All of a sudden, Sanna's not sure what to say. This seemed like a clear plan yesterday. Now she's not so sure.

"I'm just on my way to give a lecture in my Introductory Religions class," Dr. Seigel offers. "Would you like to sit in on the class and we can talk after?"

"Yes, thank you," Sanna says, grateful that Hadassah intuits what she wants.

"It's in Lowen Hall. Room 214. It starts at nine. Do you know where that is? Can you get there by then?"

"Yes. Sure," Sanna says. "I'm not far away."

"Good," says Dr. Seigel. "See you soon."

"Okay, thanks," Sanna says, and after she hangs up, she deletes the call from the girl's phone and puts it back on the table next to the laptop where the girl is now considering brown ankle boots.

"Thanks again," Sanna says.

"No problem," says the blonde girl.

No problem. As Sanna makes her way out of the coffee shop and through the small quad on campus, she wonders what it would be like to be that girl, browsing boots in a coffee shop instead of worrying about a mother detained by the government. Girls like that probably didn't even read the news. "Well, most people don't read the news anymore," Sanna hears her mother saying. "That's the problem."

No problem. That's the problem.

13.

"I am going to do a little experiment," Dr. Seigel says. "Do not be afraid." She has a slight accent that Sanna can't place. When she switches off the lights in the classroom, suddenly all the students who have been looking at their phones look up.

From the back of the room, Sanna sees dozens of phones glowing in the dark. Some turn them off right away; others just look up, not having heard Dr. Seigel's announcement, wondering what's going on.

"These lights," Dr. Seigel says, "are the signs of the brokenness of the world. Each one of us is a part of the light that was once part of the wholeness of the creator. According to the Kabbalah, the creator placed pieces of his light into vessels that shattered to create the world. In doing so, he created us, but he also limited himself."

Dr. Seigel turns the lights back on.

A boy at the front of the classroom with big glasses says, "Are you saying that God is in our phones?"

Students laugh. But Sanna feels it's a nervous laugh, like they might actually believe that.

"No." She smiles. "But that's an interesting question. Our focus for today is the concept of *tikkun olam*, which is a Judaic philosophy that encourages making the world whole again."

Sanna's ears perk up when she hears this. Her mother taught her that Cherokee ritual was also about recreating the wholeness and balance of the world.

"Let me ask you this," Dr. Seigel says. "How much power do you think you have?"

"It depends on how long my battery on my phone lasts," quips a redheaded boy from the back row as he waves his phone in the air. "And whether I get a left or right swipe."

The class laughs. Dr. Seigel nods and smiles in that way that adults have of showing they don't think something is funny. Sanna doesn't think he is funny, either. She detests boys like that.

"Could you, for example," Dr. Seigel says, "save a life?"

"Like with CPR? I learned it from the Red Cross when my baby sister was born," says a girl to Sanna's left wearing a sorority sweatshirt. With no hood.

"Maybe," says Dr. Seigel. "Are there other ways? Other ways to save a life?"

The class is silent. Dr. Seigel looks at Sanna in the back of the room as if she's going to speak to her, and then looks away.

"What if someone is jailed wrongfully?" Dr. Seigel asks. "What if you helped that person escape? Would that be right?"

"It depends on why they were in jail," says an African-American boy.

"But isn't it wrong to break the law?" the boy with black glasses at the front of the room asks.

"Exactly," says Dr. Seigel. "Those are both very good questions."

No one says anything. Sanna sees some of them disengage, go back to their phones. *Maybe God really is in the phones*, Sanna thinks. *Or maybe they think so.*

Dr. Seigel goes to the white board and writes *tikkun olam* on it.

"Repair of the world," she says. "Or construction for eternity. It goes back to those shattered vessels. If each one of us is part of the whole, then each one of us is responsible for that whole. And in turn, what one does helps create the world."

Dr. Seigel pauses.

"There is a double-edged sword in this," Dr. Seigel says, and Sanna swears she's looking right at her. "If each of us helps create the world, then it also means that what each person does has the power to either heal or destroy."

"I don't know," says the redheaded boy. "You have to have power to affect change. Not everyone has that power."

"Keep going," Dr. Seigel encourages him. "Say more."

"I mean, maybe rich people have that power. Maybe the president. Politicians. People who other people follow. But one person? Without power?"

"That is the question, isn't it?" says Dr. Seigel. "It goes back to the vessels. And the light."

"Isn't this just another version of the Eve story?" asks a girl with an asymmetrical haircut to Sanna's left. "Just another story of the fall, of brokenness?"

"Good point," says Dr. Seigel and smiles at her. "Except that in this story, we are not banished from the garden. We still have the shards of light within us."

No one says anything. Dr. Seigel looks at the clock on the wall. There are ten more minutes left in the ninety-minute class.

"One person can make a difference," she says. "If I let you out ten minutes early, your whole life could be different."

The class perks up at this, looking hopeful.

"Go ahead," she says. "Go. Make a difference."

Sanna is shocked at how quickly the electronic devices are swallowed by backpacks and pockets as bodies abandon the room.

The asymmetrical haircut girl is talking to Dr. Seigel, saying something about the free market and Adam Smith, and Dr. Seigel says,

"That's right. I'd like to talk to you about that, but I have another appointment now. How about next time?"

The girl glares at Sanna in the back of the room as she heads out the door, clearly jealous of the time she will be spending with her favorite professor.

"Sanna," Dr. Seigel asks, "what did you think of today's class?"

"My mom would agree with it."

"Indeed she would. Come to my office with me and we will talk more."

14.

They don't say anything to each other as they cross the quad and walk to the theology faculty office building. For a second, Sanna worries about running into Parker but then remembers that Parker would never teach a morning class just in case her writing is going well that day.

Dr. Seigel unlocks her office door and turns on a lamp that emits a soft yellow glow. She doesn't touch the florescent ceiling lights but plugs in a pot and says, "Tea? I have all kinds. It's almost a fetish."

Sanna peruses the dozens of flavors—sees chamomile, jasmine, green, chai, and orange— and then chooses a mint chocolate.

"Good choice," Dr. Seigel says, opting for ginger. "Have a seat," she says as she opens the tea and places the bags into two blue ceramic mugs, obviously handmade.

Sanna looks and there are two nice chairs, not the requisite faculty chairs, but real furniture with soft fabric and accent cushions. She sits down.

"Thank you for seeing me, Dr. Seigel," she says.

The water in the pot is already gurgling, and as she pours the boiling water into the ceramic mugs, Dr. Seigel says, "Call me Hadassah, please," and hands one of the mugs to Sanna.

"Hadassah," says Sanna. "What does it mean?"

"Nothing special. It's a myrtle tree in Hebrew."

"Hebrew? Are you from Israel?"

"Yes. My parents were friends with one of the founders, after the war. They were both very political. It's why I became a theologian." She smiles. "We often choose very different paths than our parents. Are you an artist like your mother?"

"No," says Sanna.

"A poet like Parker?"

"No."

Hadassah smiles again. "A practical girl?"

"Yes," Sanna admits. "Kind of normal. Boring, I guess."

Hadassah nods. "What you're going through now is not boring. It must be upsetting."

Sanna takes a chance and dives in to what she came to do.

"Parker said you know something that could hurt my mom."

Hadassah's eyebrows rise almost to her short grey, cropped hair.

"Parker doesn't know I'm here," Sanna continues. "I'm supposed to be at school. I used someone else's phone in the coffee shop to call you. Parker talked to this lawyer who said we shouldn't do anything out of the ordinary, that it could hurt my mom, but I don't understand why my mom called you and not me yesterday." The words come out of Sanna's mouth in a rush and she stops as her voice cracks, not wanting to cry.

"I understand," says Hadassah. "That must be very upsetting." She waits, takes a sip of her ginger tea.

Sanna wishes she would volunteer more. She doesn't quite know what questions to ask. She doesn't want Parker to be right, she doesn't want to hurt her mom, but she needs to know more about what's happening. What's going to happen.

"Do you believe in the *tikkun olam*?" Sanna asks.

"Yes. Yes, I do."

"That one person can save the world?"

"Yes," Hadassah repeats. "I think your mom does, too."

Sanna sips her mint chocolate tea and wonders where her mom is right now, what she is doing. Sanna can't imagine how her mom must be feeling, not able to make art. "Her art," she says. "My mom thinks of her art in that way."

"That's right."

Sanna realizes that Hadassah is not giving her any real information. She's just agreeing with whatever Sanna says. It's time to be more direct.

"Why did my mom call you?" Sanna says finally.

Hadassah puts her tea down, puts her hands together and strums her fingers, once, twice. Thinking. Considering.

"Before your mom left for the Netherlands," she says, "she had just finished an important work of art. No one had seen it yet. She worked on it alone, in her studio here on campus, with the door locked. She told me about it. I assume she told Parker. But no one had seen it. She felt it was a very important work and she was waiting for the right time to reveal it."

Hadassah picks up her tea again, holds it in front of her like a chalice. "Your mom feels very strongly that this art work needs to be preserved, so she called me to do that. To hide it."

"That was more important than me?" Sanna blurts.

"She knew Parker would be there to protect you. Someone needed to protect the art."

"Parker," Sanna says, shaking her head. "That's the problem. That's all she wants to do, protect the family. Be the world's best mom. But I need *my* mom."

Hadassah says nothing as Sanna wipes a tear away.

"If I can't see my mom, can I at least see her art?" Sanna asks.

"No."

"Why not?"

"Parker is right. That lawyer is right. We cannot do anything that might jeopardize your mother."

"But you said one person could …," Sanna starts.

"One person can. That person is me. And I'm telling you no."

15.

Sanna slams her backpack on the floor as she enters the house that afternoon. It's so loud that Nick takes his earbuds out.

"Where have you been?" he asks.

"Around," she says quietly. "Parker's not home?" She saw Parker's car in the driveway but not her mother's truck.

"No. She went to get the oil changed on your mom's truck. You know her, the way she keeps to her schedules."

Sanna sighs and flops onto the couch beside him.

"Crappy day off, Ferris Bueller?" he asks, and she smiles. It's their favorite movie to watch together.

"Yeah." She sighs again.

"Where did you go? I saw Jenny and she said you didn't show up for a ride this morning."

"I went to see Hadassah Seigel."

"That woman your mom called?"

"Yeah."

"Why?"

"I wanted to know why mom called her first. Instead of me. Seems it has to do with some art my mom made. I don't know. I spent the day walking around town and listening to the latest Tori Amos album on Spotify." Tori Amos is one of her mom's favorite singers, and Sanna wanted to feel closer to her by listening to the music.

"That's pretty emo, Squirta." He smiles.

It makes her smile. Laugh, even.

"I know. But the album is pretty good, actually."

"Emo extra," he says, and they both laugh.

"If you ask me, which you didn't, because I'm only your older, wiser, better-looking brother and all, but if you ask me, you're asking the wrong question."

"What? About Tori Amos?"

"No. About going to see that woman."

"What do you mean?"

"Think of it this way," he says, pointing at the laptop. "What you find on a search engine has everything to do with what you're looking for."

"So?"

"So you asked her the wrong question."

"What do you mean?"

"You wanted to know why. The real question is what."

"Nick, I have no idea what you're talking about," Sanna says and grimaces.

"You asked that woman *why* your mom called her. What you really want to know is *what* she said."

"Huh."

"What is an infinitely more helpful question," he says. "It was actually your mom who taught me that."

"Really?"

"Yep. When I was in middle school these kids were bullying me."

"I remember that."

"And your mom said she learned something from her therapist that really helped her," Nick tells her.

"What?"

"Exactly," he says, and smiles, crosses his arms like he's finished.

She punches him lightly. "Stop it," she says.

"Nah, I'm just playing. What she said is that her therapist taught her to ask herself, 'What am I going to do about it?'"

Sanna thinks about this. Yes, that is actually what she was trying to ask Hadassah but she asked the wrong question.

"Tembe told me," Nick continues, "that when something bad is happening, we can get caught up in our reaction, how we feel about it, and this can just sink us deeper into the muck. She said that Cecie taught her that asking 'What am I going to do about it?' is the solution."

"What am I going to do about it?" Sanna says, almost whispering, lost in thinking.

"What, Squirta, are you going to do about it?"

Sanna thinks for a minute.

"I'm going to call Cecie," she says.

"Want help?" he asks.

It doesn't take long for him to find Cecie's number. Nick looks it up for her on his laptop and messages it to her phone. She presses the number, then goes into her room for privacy, leaving Nick, who is already putting his earbuds back in, his brotherly advice for the day having been given.

The voice mail comes on.

She leaves a message. "This is Sanna Penbrook. I'm Tembe's daughter. I'd like to talk to you about," she hesitates and then says, "I'd like to talk to you about *what* I can do to help my mom." She gives her number and sits down to wait, then remembers she has missed two days of school in a row, and the next day is Friday. And she has two tests.

About two hours later, after reviewing for tests on quadratic equations and oligarchy, the phone rings.

"Hello?"

"Sanna?"

"Yes."

"This is Cecie Kingston. You wanted to speak with me?"

"Yes. Um, I … could I come see you?"

There is a moment when Sanna thinks she might say no.

"Sure. How about after school tomorrow?"

Sanna breathes a sigh of relief.

"Perfect. Thank you," she says.

16.

Cecie Kingston is a petite African-American woman with short, natural hair and a soft smile. She welcomes Sanna into her office on that Friday afternoon after school and offers her some tea.

But this time, unlike with Hadassah, Sanna says no. She is more focused now. More determined this time. She doesn't want to be sidetracked. She feels the fierce spirit of her mother rising in her.

"You look so much like your mom," Cecie says.

"Thanks," Sanna says. "I get that a lot."

"Spitting image, my grandma would say." Cecie smiles.

It makes Sanna smile, and then she refocuses. "I'm here because you know my mom," she says. She thinks back to what Nick told her. To focus on the reason she's here. To focus on the what. What she can do to help her mom.

After explaining the ONE policy and her mother's detention to Cecie, Sanna says again, "You know my mom. I think you know what she would want me to do. I feel like I just have to do something. I want to help my mom."

Cecie nods. "What have you done so far?"

"I talked to Parker, and she says we can't do anything. She said she called a good lawyer and he advised her that we shouldn't do anything that might jeopardize my mom. But that doesn't sound like a solution to me. Just wait? While my mom is in jail, basically?"

"What do you think Parker was feeling when she gave you that advice?" Cecie asks.

That's a good question, Sanna thinks. She hadn't thought of that.

"Fear, I guess," Sanna says.

Cecie nods. "And when we are afraid, what do we usually do?"

"Hide."

Cecie nods again. "But you don't want to hide?"

"No," says Sanna emphatically. "I'm not really afraid. I'm actually kind of angry. I wanted to know why my mom called Hadassah Seigel first instead of us. So I stole Hadassah's number from Parker's phone and called her and went to see her."

"Was that wrong?" It isn't an admonition, just a question.

"No," says Sanna, thinking back to Hadassah's lecture. "There is wrong and right and sometimes what seems to be wrong according to a rule is the right thing."

"Why was it right?" Cecie asks gently. She is very good at this, Sanna thinks. She asks good questions.

"It was right because I do not think being afraid and hiding are what my mom would want me to do."

"Do you always do what your mom wants you to do?"

Sanna smiles. "Of course not. I mean, I'm a normal kid. But …."

"But?" Cecie encourages her to continue.

"But I'm a kid! And I don't want to be. I went to talk to Hadassah and she talked about this Jewish concept, that one person can make a difference in the world. It's called *tikkun olam*. And I know my mom believes that. I believe it. She raised me to believe it when she taught me about the Cherokee beliefs in the wholeness of the world. But Hadassah wouldn't let me see my mom's art. She thinks it could incriminate her or something. I don't know. I just …."

"Just what, Sanna?" Cecie asks kindly.

"I'm just so tired of everything!" Sanna blurts. "My moms are talking about politics constantly, and I swear they are addicted to Rachel Maddow, it's like their religion or something, and I knew it was getting bad for a lot of people, I knew it would probably get worse, but I didn't think it would actually come to this. I had no idea that my mom would end up in jail!"

Cecie takes a deep breath, exhales slowly.

"No one ever thinks that something like this will happen," she says. "Even when it's happened before, even to your own people in the past."

Sanna nods. Their moms have taught Nick and her more about African-American history than the public schools ever would. And for some reason she thinks about the trip they took to D.C. to visit the new museum a month before the election.

"Do you know about Ashley's sack?" Sanna asks, and Cecie's eyes crinkle with curiosity as she shakes her head no.

"We went on a family trip to the African-American history museum in D.C. before the election. It seems so long ago now. Another world."

Cecie nods.

"And there was something in the museum that struck me that I've never forgotten. It was a feed sack that had been embroidered by a woman named Ruth. Her grandmother, Rose, during slavery, had filled the sack with gifts for her nine-year old daughter Ashley when she was sold away. Pecans. A tattered dress. A lock of her hair. And all her love forever."

Cecie's eyes fill with tears as she listens intensely.

"The daughter Ashley passed this story, and the sack, down to her daughter, Ruth, who embroidered the story of it onto the fabric."

Cecie waits as Sanna looks out the window, thinking.

"I want to be like Ruth. I want to do something so people see what has happened. What is happening. What can I do?"

Cecie nods, and now it is her turn to look out the window. She is clearly considering something. She is contemplating her *what*.

"Did your mom ever tell you about The ReSisters?" Cecie asks quietly, almost whispering.

"No."

"It's a group. An underground women's group. Your mom is a member. But Parker is not."

Sanna is surprised. Parker and her mom do everything together.

"Does Parker even know about it?" Sanna asks, thinking about Parker's caution, her fear, the call to the lawyer.

"Yes," Cecie says. "She does. But she's not a member. She doesn't believe in some of their methods."

"Are you?"

"No."

"How can I find out more about it? Do you think I can I join them? Do you think they might help me help my mom?"

Cecie thinks for a minute. It feels like a long minute to Sanna.

Then she says, "I think you should ask Parker. She will know who else is in the group. And she's your mother. She will know what's best for you. And if you disagree with her, or if she won't tell you what you want to know ... well, you'll need to have a dialogue. You need to come to some agreement. That's what all this is about, isn't it? People needing to come to a shared understanding? Isn't that what Ruth did with her embroidery? Help people understand what otherwise might have been forgotten?"

17.

"Parker, I need to talk to you," Sanna says that evening, as Parker stirs the spaghetti sauce on the stove for dinner.

"Okay. What is it?"

"Not here," Sanna says, and flashes her eyes toward the living room where Nick is. "Outside."

After Parker turns the stove off, they go out the back door to the yard. There are yellow and red and orange leaves all over the ground. Tembe would have been raking them that weekend, maybe even that very afternoon, had she come home. She loved yard work and always looked forward to the weekend when she could be outside from dawn to dusk.

Loves, Sanna corrects herself internally. It's not like she's dead. There's no reason to think of her in the past tense.

"What is it, Sanna?" Parker asks, pulling her back to the present.

"I don't want to keep secrets from you," Sanna says. "I went to see Hadassah."

"What?"

"Yes. But don't worry. She didn't let me see the art. So it's safe." There is an edge to Sanna's voice. "And I also went to see Cecie today."

"Cecie? Your mom's therapist?"

"Yes. I wanted to ask her advice. About what I could do. For mom."

"I see. I know she helped your mom a great deal. Did she help you?"

"She told me about The ReSisters."

Parker takes a sharp breath. "She did?"

"Yes. And she said you're not a part of it, but you know about it. You could tell me how to find out more."

"Oh, Sanna, I really don't think this is a good idea." Parker crosses her arms in front of her, as if putting up a shield.

"Parker," Sanna almost shouts, "I have to do something! I am going to go crazy if I just sit around doing nothing to help while my mom is in jail!"

"But Dixon says—"

"Nick said that guy is a scum bag," Sanna argues. "You yourself said he's a friend of Nick's dad, who is also apparently not a good guy. So we're supposed to take the advice of a someone like that? While my mom is in trouble? You know that's not what my mom would want us to do!"

Parker looks down at the ground. She kicks at a few dried leaves with her foot. Sanna can tell she's talking with Tembe in her mind, almost as if Tembe is in those leaves, and Parker's trying to get her to speak. Sanna knows that Parker knows that Tembe would encourage Sanna's desire to do something. To be courageous. To rise up. To resist.

"Okay," Parker says finally. "There's a friend of ours that I know. Eden. I know she's in the group. Your mom didn't tell me who all the members are, but I know Eden is one. She works at the campus arboretum. Maybe you could go see her. But don't call her, okay? We don't want a digital record of that, do you understand? You can go to the arboretum tomorrow."

She pauses. Looks around the yard. There are so many leaves. The grass is completely hidden underneath. Parker sighs.

"You can go tomorrow after you and Nick help me rake these leaves," she says. "Tembe would want us to do that. Keep up with the chores. After we finish the yard work, you can go, okay? Eden is always there. I'm sure you'll be able to talk to her."

"Okay," Sanna says. "Thank you, Parker."

"I'm just so worried," Parker says, and her eyes fill with tears.

"I know," Sanna says. "Me, too." And because she feels bad for Parker, because she knows Parker is as unmoored without Tembe as she is, she hugs her. And, for a second, Sanna feels her mother's strength within her once again.

It makes Parker smile.

"Thank you, honey," she says. "I really needed that hug."

"Me, too," says Sanna. And it's true.

"Now let's go in and eat," Parker says. "I've made such a good dinner!" She has regained her usual cheerfulness.

Sanna thinks about what Hadassah taught her about one person making a difference. She certainly made a difference to Parker by offering her that hug.

And Sanna thinks about what Cecie said about coming to a shared understanding. Not only the hug did that, but their talk, outside, here, in the yard with the fallen leaves, and Sanna standing up and saying what she wanted. All of that did that.

The pieces of it, all of it, how each woman shared something different with her and made her think in a new way reminds Sanna of the story of the shattered vessels with light in them. Maybe Parker and Hadassah and Cecie are all, in their own ways, pieces of her mother.

Not that her mother is shattered. Sanna refuses to believe that.

But that there's somehow some kind of wholeness that can be recovered in the world when women work together.

She will know more tomorrow. When she meets Eden. When she finds out more about The ReSisters.

For the first time in days, Sanna smiles a real smile. Parker notices it and thinks she's smiling in anticipation of her spaghetti dinner and smiles back. Sweet Parker. It really takes so little to make her happy. And they really are on the same side. Her mother would tell her not to believe the patriarchal myths about evil stepmothers, that it's just a way to keep women from different generations from uniting against the father figure. This makes Sanna smile even wider. Parker puts her arm around Sanna. And they go inside.

18.

After helping Parker and Nick rake the leaves in the back yard, which takes them all morning and some of the afternoon, Sanna hops in the shower and gets ready to go to the arboretum.

Nick drives Parker's car and drops her off at the front gate.

"Good luck," he says as she steps out of the car. "See you in an hour." She doesn't know how much he knows about what she's going to do, but she suspects he knows even more than she does.

"Thanks, bro," Sanna says and steps through the wrought iron fence into the hilly forest.

It's cooler here where the late afternoon November sun doesn't reach, hidden by the tall trunks and broad branches of poplar, sweetgum and loblolly pine trees.

It's quiet, too. Sanna can hear the crunch her feet make as she steps over the fallen leaves. No one rakes here, and the path is barely visible. She follows it.

There is a small wooden building, not much more than a shed, about four hundred yards inside the gate, and Sanna starts to knock and then realizes the door is open and a woman is sitting on the floor in a meditation posture, eyes closed. She has waist-long light brown hair that covers her shoulders like a cloak.

Sanna is sure she has heard her approach and doesn't want to bother her. For a second, she thinks about leaving, and then the woman opens her eyes and says, "Welcome."

"I'm sorry. I didn't mean to disturb you," Sanna says.

"You didn't. I'm Eden. How can I help you?"

The question echoes in Sanna's head. Eden is offering *tikkun olam* even though she doesn't realize it. They hear an owl hoot from a high tree, and Eden says, "They're nesting nearby. And the babies must be hungry."

Sanna nods. "I'm Sanna Penbrook. I think you know my mother, Tembe?"

Eden stands. "Yes." She smiles. "I heard about what's happened. I'm sorry."

"You know?"

"I know. You want to go for a walk? I'd love to show you around."

Sanna is doing a lot of talking and walking these days, she thinks, and says, "Sure."

They don't talk for a while as Eden leads her deeper into the shade of the arboretum. The sky is that deep sapphire of November through the few leaves still clinging to the trees. It is peaceful here. Sanna can almost forget why she's there.

"It's peaceful here," Eden says quietly, as if she can read her mind.

"Yes," Sanna says. "But it's not out there."

"No, it's not. But it could be."

"How?"

Sanna realizes she has asked the why and the what, but this is the first time she has asked how.

Eden reaches her hands out to gesture toward the woods. "Did you know that at one time all of this was covered in fields of cotton?"

"No," says Sanna.

"It's true. Every step we take on the land carries history under our feet."

Sanna nods. It sounds like something her mother would say.

"But that history did not just end," continues Eden. "Someone had to take action. To stop slavery. It took a war. But it happened."

Sanna is not quite sure what Eden's getting at. Is she saying they need to start a war?

"It has to be collective," Eden says.

"I don't really know what you mean," Sanna says. "I was wondering if I could ask you about something. I heard you're in a group with my mother. Is it a collective? Is that what you mean?"

"Yes," Eden says and then pauses. "Come sit." She gestures to a wooden bench a bit away from the path, surrounded by cypress knees.

They sit. Eden takes a slow breath.

"Form is important in times of crisis," she says. "Look at these cypress knees. They are roots. But they grow above ground because the soil is so swampy. They realize their form has to take a different shape than regular roots."

Sanna can see how her mom would be friends with this woman. She speaks about nature the way her mom speaks about art.

"In the old days," Eden continues, "collective action was visible. That was the form it took in order to be effective. Protests, marching in the streets, demonstrations. Sit-ins, boycotts. These could work, not always effectively, but at least incrementally, because everyone was in the same element."

Eden reaches down and picks up a brown caterpillar. "Change happens slowly in nature," she says. "And it's visible if you look close enough."

Sanna wonders if she's a caterpillar now. If what is happening is just part of growing.

"But what is happening now is not natural," Eden says, again answering her silent questions out loud. "What is happening is not natural, and in some ways it's not even human."

"Not human?"

"It's the result of networks. Technologies. Large corporations that put systems in motion and have lost control of them."

Sanna waits. She's still not clear about what Eden is saying.

"It's not clear," Eden continues, echoing her thoughts again. "It's not something you can point to or trace very clearly. It's underground. That's why we have to work underground. The ReSisters don't work in the normal ways that groups do."

"Is that why my mom was detained? Because they found out she was a member of the group?"

"Maybe," says Eden. "The why doesn't matter. The guards, the officers, you see, they are not humans anymore. They have become part of the system, untethered to a natural ecosystem, unmoored from their roots, and not even certain of what branch of the tree they are on. Not even knowing what the tree is."

Sanna takes a deep breath.

"How did this happen?" Sanna asks. She thinks about the photo of her mom on the internet. How she has no idea who took that picture, or how it got there.

"People forgot about all this," Eden says, waving her hand toward the forest. "This is just an arboretum now. An enclosed space, like a museum, to help us remember what the world used to be."

Sanna nods. "My mom says that about Cherokee. That it's become a tourist place. It's not what it was. It's not even where they lived in the past."

"That's right. We're living in a time of symbols. The real is only pointed at with signs."

"How do we know what is right?" Sanna asks, thinking of Parker's desire to mother and protect, Hadassah's desire to heal the world, and Cecie's belief in dialogue and understanding. She also thinks of her mother's adherence to art as a way of telling the truth. She wonders what Eden's answer will be.

Eden is quiet for a long time.

Longer than Sanna is comfortable.

They hear the wind rustling through the leaves on the forest floor. They feel a slight dip in temperature as the sun tips lower in the west. The light shifts.

Sanna realizes this is Eden's answer. Silence. The silence of nature.

She is not sure what she's going to do with that. She is pretty sure that this forest can't save her mother.

"You have to get quiet for a long time," Eden says finally, very softly. "The more upset you are, the worse things seem to be, the quieter you need to be, for longer. This is where the human is. In the silence of a listening heart."

And when Eden says that, Sanna begins to cry for the first time about her mother. Tears of a child. Abandoned. Snatched. Like one of the children taken by Spearfinger.

She thinks back to Halloween afternoon, when she put her costume on. She feels somehow that Spearfinger entered her life at that moment. And her tears take on a different consistency. In the midst of grief, Sanna is gripped, as if by one long, sharp, knifelike finger, by terror.

And Eden takes the child in her arms and holds her.

19.

Nick pulls up to the gate of the arboretum at their appointed time. The lights on Parker's Subaru are bright in the gathering darkness, and almost blinding as Sanna waits for him.

She opens the door to the car and says, "Eden has invited us to dinner with her and her husband. She wants to tell us more about this group that my mom's in, but she can't invite us to a meeting, so she wants us to come to dinner."

Nick's eyes get wide. "You know Parker isn't going to like that," he says.

"I know. What do you want to do?" she asks, a light smile on her face as she recalls the question he taught her, from her mom, to ask. She also knows he is usually interested in an adventure.

"Hold up," he says, and takes out his phone. Sanna watches as he texts Parker.

"Sanna wants to go out for pizza with me. Ok?" he types and hits send.

They wait a second. "Sounds good," Parker texts back.

Sanna thinks about what Eden said to her, about the systems and networks. Somewhere between Nick's text to his mom and her text back, a system has been set in motion, and it's getting harder to figure out what is a lie and what is the truth, what is right and what is wrong.

Sanna flops into the seat of the car and says, "I have the address written on paper. I'm not supposed to put it on my phone. Do you know where Carrboro is?"

"Sure."

"Good. She said it's across from the graveyard on Route 501 as you're entering Carrboro. It shouldn't be hard to find."

Nick revs the engine, as much as someone can rev a Subaru, and says, "Going to learn more about the underground resistance across from a cemetery on a full moon night? This should be fun."

On the way, as they stop for flowers at a grocery store because their mothers taught them never to visit someone's house for dinner without a gift, Sanna fills him in on the conversations she's been having. Somehow with that text to his mother, he has allied himself with Sanna, and as she explains what she's learned from Hadassah and Cecie and Eden, she realizes that maybe Parker was wrong about needing to protect him from all this information because he seems calmer as he listens, as if missing puzzle pieces are falling into place.

The house is a cute two-story bungalow right across from the graveyard as Eden described, and their Jack O'lanterns are lit on the porch along with dozens of candles on the railings and hanging from the ceiling. The moon is rising in the east to the left of the house, and Sanna is reminded again of the lessons about the shards of light that Hadassah taught her.

"Welcome," calls a man from the porch, holding a long lighter and wearing jeans and a white button-down shirt.

"Thanks," says Nick. "I'm Nick and this is Sanna."

"I'm Asher."

They all shake hands and Asher leads them into the house.

"Merry meet," Eden calls from the kitchen, and Nick and Sanna are not quite sure what to say, so they say, "Hey."

Soon she is coming into the living room with a tray of steaming drinks. She's changed from the jeans she was wearing at the arboretum and her long hair is up in a messy bun that makes her look kind of magical.

"Hunter Moon Apple Cider," she says. "Just a hint of rum." She winks, and everyone takes one.

The taste is sweet and spicy, and the rum warms her belly long after Sanna swallows. They gather near a fire pit on the side of the house, and Sanna can see the moon rising on her left and the graveyard across the street on her right. At first the talk is mundane. Weather. Local sports teams. The recent World Series. Sanna finds it odd that Asher and Nick are doing most of the talking when they are ostensibly here to learn more about The ReSisters.

She wonders if Asher doesn't even know why they are there. She wants to know why Eden is being so quiet.

"Do you need any help in the kitchen?" she asks Eden. She has seen her moms do this when they have people over and one of them wants to talk to the other privately.

"Sure," says Eden, and they go in.

"Want more?" Eden asks, refilling her mug from a pot on the stove.

"No, thanks," says Sanna. "One is enough for me." Her mom doesn't drink much and Sanna knows that her grandmother was an alcoholic who died from liver failure, and, although she's had beer and wine coolers at a few parties, she doesn't like it much.

"Does Asher know about The ReSisters?" Sanna blurts.

"Sure," Eden laughs. "He used to be one."

"What?"

"I didn't think you knew. And I didn't want to say anything in front of him. I usually like to let him tell people. Asher is trans."

"Trans?"

"You know, transgender. When someone transitions from one gender to another. Asher used to be Ashley. We were gay. We were old married lesbians even before it was legal. Now I'm married to a man and I'm straight and that's as legal as it gets these days." She laughs again, "So I guess I transitioned, too. Not that I had a choice."

"Didn't you?"

"What?"

"Have a choice?"

"Well, no. Not really. When you're young, you think you always have choices. Liberal feminists, of course, are all about freedom of choice. Women can enter the military now. Even in combat positions. That's a liberating choice, they say. But I don't think it works that way. I am beginning to think maybe the astrophysicists are right, that's there's not a choice, there's just patterns of motion."

Sanna can't quite follow what she's saying. Maybe it's the cider, or maybe Eden isn't really making sense, even to herself. She watches as Eden downs a second mug of cider and pours a third one and then takes a casserole out of the oven.

"I wanted to let Asher talk to Nick tonight because there's a lot of guy stuff he doesn't get to do, you know, with people who knew him as Ashley. They see two people. Nick can see him as one. As united with himself."

"The Cherokee say gay people are two-spirits," Sanna offers. "My mom told me that. There's nothing wrong with being more than one."

Eden nods, and says, "That's right. Cool."

Once they are seated around the oval table in the dining room, which is just a corner between the kitchen and the living room, Eden serves up the casserole, a mix of winter vegetables in a luscious cream sauce, along with crusty bread and a big salad. Sanna's mom would love this meal, and Parker would love to have the recipe. But this is one meal that she won't be sharing with them.

Asher is not done dominating the conversation, it seems, because now he's describing, mostly to Nick, his new job at a think tank in the Research Triangle and how the international markets are breaking down, no longer relying upon old classifications between first and third world nations now that multinational corporations are in just about every place on earth.

"Asher, honey," Eden interrupts, "Sanna is here to see if she can help her mom. She wants to know more about The ReSisters, not about the global market."

Asher looks down and Sanna can see a trace of the female in the way he feels admonished, however lightly, by Eden. And then he looks up.

"Here's the thing. It's a good group. It has good intentions. But it's basically a colonial country. That's what I was trying to get at," he says, shooting a look at Eden. "The lines of power are being redrawn. And The ReSisters are relying on old models of gender and power. Do you let the colonialists define your identity even in a postcolonial society? Why shouldn't I still be part of the group now that I identify as a man? What is real femininity and masculinity? It doesn't exist."

Sanna interrupts him. "But I still don't get what they do."

Eden takes over. "The ReSisters are partly a resurgence of a feminist group in this area from the seventies. There are a bunch of older women in it who have successfully created new institutions, especially in art and publishing, that led to major changes in our society."

"But they use the old paradigms," says Asher.

"Let me finish," says Eden, and then turns back to Sanna. "And there are women your mom's age and mine who are kind of the transitional—" She stops and grins at Asher, maybe as a way to make peace. "We provide the bridge between the older activists and the younger generation."

"How would you characterize the younger generation?" asks Sanna.

"Good question," says Eden. "They don't like names. Or labels of any kind."

"That is the way the world is going," says Asher.

"It's almost like they're playing at feminism, though," says Eden. "It's like everything is ironic because nothing can be trusted."

"Nothing can be trusted," says Nick, speaking for the first time, and they all stare at him for a moment.

"This administration is out of control," Nick continues. "But it's not them. It's not, like, just the head." He looks at Asher. "What you were saying makes a lot of sense. I've been lurking on this 8space site, and you wouldn't believe how many people actually want authoritarianism."

"But how many of them are even real Americans and not Russian bots?" Eden asks.

"What does it matter?" Nick and Asher say almost simultaneously.

"This is what I was trying to say," says Asher. "The nation as we know it is over, just as gender is over. They still exist, but they're not essences. They are performances that fit specific situations and then can morph again. The only essential thing is power."

Eden drops her fork. "And who has the most power?" Eden asks, looking directly at him.

Sanna can tell this is an old argument. She watches as Asher takes his fork and points it at Eden, saying, "Men. Not always and not forever, but for right now. Men."

No one speaks for a minute and then Nick's phone rings. It's his mom.

20.

"Mom?" Nick says as the rest of the people at the table stay quiet.

Sanna can hear her voice, even from across the table. "Nicky! I have such good news! Put me on speaker. I want your sister to hear."

For a second, Sanna is nervous about this. These are not family, and Parker doesn't know where they are, but Nick clicks the speaker button and says, "Go ahead."

"I just got a call from Dixon," she says.

"On a Saturday night?" Nick asks, and Sanna is afraid. But Parker said it's good news. She feels she can't wait any longer.

"What is it?" Sanna asks, her voice shaking.

"Honey," Parker says, "Your mom has been transferred to a local education facility. They were just keeping her in the New York center for processing, but she's here, now. Outside of Raleigh. And tomorrow is visiting day! We can go see her!"

"Mom, that's great news," Nick says, and Sanna can tell he's not sure about having this news shared among relative strangers, either. "Listen, Mom, we'll be home soon, okay?"

"Okay, good. I'm just so excited!"

"Me, too, Mom. See you soon."

No one speaks at the table as Eden gets up to clear the dishes.

Finally, Asher says, almost yelling toward the kitchen, "Are you going to tell them or should I?"

In a flash, Eden is out of the kitchen saying, "Well, now someone will, won't they?"

"What?" says Nick.

Eden takes a deep breath, sighs, and says, "There's a demonstration planned by The ReSisters at the detention center tomorrow. Well, technically, it's a counter protest because there's going to be a pro-ONE rally outside the detention center since it's visiting day, and they want to intimidate the families of the detainees."

"Well, that will be intimidating," says Sanna.

"You could join us?" offers Eden.

Without thinking, Sanna says, "I'll be there to see my mom. There's no way I'm going to miss that by standing around with a sign and risking getting arrested."

Nick smiles.

Asher does, too. "See, dear?" he says. "The young are the future of the movement."

Sanna's not sure if he's making fun of her, but Nick gives them an out by saying, "We better get going. Thank you so much for dinner. It was delicious."

They walk to the porch and Asher has his arm around Eden. She walks away from him and toward Sanna and grasps both her hands just before they get to the car.

"No matter what happens tomorrow," she says. "I hope you get to see your mom."

21.

"What the hell did she mean by that?" Sanna says as soon as the car doors are closed.

"I don't know," says Nick. "How well did your mom know these people?"

"I'm not sure," says Sanna. "Cecie told me mom was in this group, and your mom let me go talk to Eden, but maybe it wasn't such a good idea to lie to your mom and accept the dinner invitation."

Nick is driving a little too fast down the highway, probably trying to get home quickly so Parker won't ask too many questions.

"At least we know what's going down tomorrow," he says.

"What do we know?" Sanna says. "We know there will be demonstrators."

"On both sides," Nick says and they both laugh even though it's not really funny. It's a way of relieving the tension.

"Can we talk about that dude back there for a minute?" he asks.

"Asher?"

"Yeah. What was his deal? He was like power hungry or something. What's such a big feminist like Eden doing with someone like that?"

"He used to be a woman," Sanna says.

"Oh, man! For real?" he exclaims.

"Yup. She told me in the kitchen."

"Well," he says, smiling, "I don't see that marriage lasting much longer."

They lapse into silence, thinking about their moms' marriage, the equal vow of it, the way even though they are different, it's always equal. Sanna thinks about what Eden said about the older feminists, the tyranny of sameness. She's lost in thought when Nick interrupts her.

"It'll be so good to see Tembe," he says, and there's a lump in his throat.

"Yeah," she says. "Your mom is going to be so happy."

These are little words. Just phrases. But they stand in for family, for their shared lives and how they are intertwined. In ways that are so much deeper than language or labels. And in that moment, Sanna knows that Asher wasn't right. There are some things that aren't just socially constructed and subject to whim in their creation and destruction.

There are some things that, with or without blood, run as deep as blood.

She and Nick and Parker and her mom are family. No doubt about it, absolutely, forever and ever.

And tomorrow, she will get to see her mom.

Nick takes 40 to get home more quickly, and Sanna can see the full moon in the passenger side rear view mirror. High in the sky now, as if it's lighting their way.

When they get home about twenty minutes later, Parker is already in bed. They stand at the foot of her bed and answer in monosyllables, as teenagers do who have been somewhere that their parents don't know about.

"How was the pizza?" Parker asks.

"Good," says Nick.

"Did you have fun?"

"Yes," says Sanna.

And then Parker squeals, "Come and give me hugs, you guys! I'm so excited about tomorrow."

As Parker kisses the top of Sanna's head, she says, "I smell smoke. Were you near a fire?"

"Brick oven pizza," says Nick.

"Oh. Well, time for night-night. I want to be up early tomorrow and make a good breakfast and hit the road. I don't know how long we'll have to wait to see her. We probably won't have much time with her. But any time ... hey, look at me, babbling while I'm trying to tell you to go to sleep."

"It's okay, Mom," Nick says. "We're excited, too."

"Oh, wait," says Parker. "I almost forgot to ask. How was your meeting with Eden?"

Sanna smiles. "Fine," she says. "She's very nice. A little kooky."

"That's what your mom thinks, too." Parker smiles and blows them a kiss good night.

They shut the bedroom door and walk down the hallway. Just in front of his bedroom, Nick tugs on Sanna's shoulder and pulls her into a hug.

"I love you, Squirta," he says suddenly.

"I love you, too, Nick," she says. She can't remember the last time he said this to her. Probably before he hit puberty. It makes her happy. It also worries her because it could be a sign that he knows more about what might happen at this demonstration tomorrow than he's letting on.

It seems like neither of them will get very much sleep that night.

Part Two

1.

Tembe wakes before dawn, before the reveille is called, and the sun feels very far away. She knows the time changed the night before but she has no idea what time it is.

It feels like freedom, even in the concrete detention center, to be able to lie under a blanket in the dark, no one barking orders, no bright lights on her, no one trying to indoctrinate her into what it means to be an American.

The sun is touching down somewhere over the Atlantic Ocean, she guesses, and she thinks of the first ships Native Americans would have seen on the eastern horizon. She read once that they did not see them at first. It was so out of the ordinary realm of their experience that their minds literally couldn't see what was coming for them.

And then a shaman warned them.

The warning created the possibility for them. And then they could see.

She pulls the scratchy government-issued space blanket closer to her chin and thinks about blankets in history. Wonders what she cannot see, in the dark of the cell and the unknowing space of her mind. What she cannot see that might be coming for her today.

Visitation. They have told her that. She will get to see her people. How long will she have? How long will the wait for them take? How will she feel, seeing their faces, knowing she will not be able to go home with them? Will it almost be worse, after they leave?

She hears Maggie, the woman in the bunk above her, shift and turn.

"Visitation day, sister," Maggie whispers. "Are you excited?"

"Yeah," Tembe says, but she is being polite. She doesn't really mean it. She doesn't mean anything in here. She has seen dogs in captivity like this, their tails wagging when someone approaches, but it is an imitation of an emotion. She closes her eyes and imagines that Sanna is in front of her, practices moving her lips into a smile, hoping she can hide the despair she feels once her daughter is really in front of her.

But even in the freedom of the pre-dawn dark, she doubts she'll be able to pull it off.

Maggie climbs down from the bunk with her pillow and takes off the case to use as a prayer rug. As Maggie begins her morning prayers, Tembe wonders about all the people in detention centers that the nation has deemed a threat. It seems to Tembe that the real threat is outside these walls. The women she has met, like Maggie, are kind and want nothing more than to live in peace. The same cannot be said about those who approve of their detention, or worse, those who ignore what is going on and live their lives as if nothing unusual is happening.

2.

"Breakfast!"

Sanna hears Parker calling them from the kitchen. Please, no eggs, she thinks, stretching under the covers and then suddenly remembering.

That's right! She gets to see her mom today. She jumps up and makes her bed.

It's pancakes. She sits at the breakfast table with a sigh of relief and says, "Thanks, Parker. These look great."

"I had the hardest time getting dressed this morning," Parker says. "I wanted to wear an outfit that Tembe had given me, but I realized that she's given me so much that I just couldn't decide."

She has settled on a green sweater, woolen tan skirt with leggings, and the turquoise boots she got from Tembe on their summer trip to Nashville when Tembe had a show at the museum on the Native American roots of country music.

"You look nice, Mom," Nick says, his mouth full of syrupy pancakes.

"Thank you, honey." She smiles at him.

Sanna's not sure how Parker can be so genuinely happy today. It's not like Tembe is coming home. Who knows how long they will even be able to see her? The pancakes have a slightly sour taste in Sanna's mouth. She doesn't take seconds.

"Not very hungry?" Parker asks.

"Too excited," says Sanna, but it's a lie. She's more nervous than excited. Her stomach hurts like it always does when she is worried. It doesn't make sense to her and she'd never admit it out loud, but she almost doesn't want to go.

After Nick finishes a second plate of pancakes, Parker gets up to wash the dishes and Nick rolls his eyes at Sanna to signal he wants to talk to her.

"We'll go get dressed," he says to Parker. "And, hey, I was thinking, maybe you could pack some sandwiches? We don't know how long we'll have to wait."

"Good idea, Nicky," Parker calls over the sound of the water running, and he and Sanna head back toward the bedroom hallway.

"What is it?" Sanna whispers.

"The demonstrations," he says.

"What about them?"

"There was something in what Eden said last night as we were leaving that got me wondering," he says.

Sanna says nothing, waits for him to continue. She can see on his face that he is hesitating.

"I stayed up last night to monitor the chat rooms in 8space," he says, slowly.

"And what?" she blurts.

"Nothing," he says, his face suddenly a book that has closed. "I didn't want you to worry. I just wanted you to know that what Asher and Eden said seems to be true. There will be demonstrations, but there should also be a big police presence."

"That's reassuring," Sanna says, shaking her head. "I'm getting in the shower first. Is that okay?" She doesn't want to hear any more about what Nick knows.

"Go ahead," he says and heads back into his room.

"I'm making a few tuna and a few turkey, plus a couple peanut butter and jelly," Parker calls from the kitchen. "That way, we'll have choices."

"Sounds good," Sanna shouts from the bathroom and smiles. Her mom is in jail, Nick's going off on conspiracy trails, but at least Parker is still so very Parkerish.

3.

After breakfast, the "citizens in training," as they are called, report to their homerooms for a debriefing about the day's visitation. The guards call themselves "teachers" and their days are divided into "classes," but it is just a jail, they are just inmates, and, Tembe thinks as she heads to her homeroom, it is weirdly a way of keeping some sense of what is happening that she remembers the correct terms for what they are, even if it is only in the space of her own mind.

"If you think you might have people coming," says the teacher/guard at the front of the classroom, "you should sign this sheet. You don't have to know who is coming, just put your name down."

The young woman, who in another universe might have been a student of Tembe's, hands the clipboard to Tembe, who signs the sheet and passes it to the woman next to her.

"When visitation time arrives, all citizens in training will wait in the eastern yard. There will be a secured area for the visits to take place."

Outside. Tembe hadn't envisioned it taking place outside.

"I must warn you that there's the possibility that the event may not be able to be executed today. We have been informed that a demonstration is planned, and security may be needed for that rather than for the visitation. It depends on the size of the crowd."

Demonstration? Tembe wonders and, for some reason, she thinks of Eden. She shakes her head, trying to dislodge the association. It makes no sense. The ReSisters work underground, they are committed to staying under the radar to create change in new ways. It wouldn't be like them to have an old-fashioned protest out in the open. Not on visitation day.

"Who is demonstrating?" asks a woman to Tembe's right.

The teacher/guard hesitates and then answers.

"ONEsters," she says. "Patriots. People supportive of what we are doing here. They want to show your loved ones that the nation approves of your education."

Sure they do, Tembe thinks. Otherwise it wouldn't be happening.

"While the clipboard goes around, I'll set up our morning video. This one is about the Christian roots of the founding of our country," the teacher/guard says, lighting up the smart board. "There will be a quiz after, so you're free to take notes."

Free. The word reverberates in Tembe's mind as she holds herself back from picking up a pencil. The urge to draw and write what she really feels would be too great.

4.

By the time they arrive, the parking lot is already full, and they have to circle back down the rural road and park alongside the ditch with hundreds of other cars. For a second, Sanna is reminded of parking for the state fair on a road like this, crossing the street holding Nick's hand as he held Parker's and she held her mom's.

Hand in hand in hand in hand. A family.

No one holds anyone else's hand today. They are too old, and each in their own way wants to be on their own taking in everything. The chants coming from the facility can be heard hundreds of yards away.

"You migrate? We educate!"

"One nation! Education!"

Sanna is sure her mom can hear this from wherever she is and she cannot bear to imagine her rage. But then, Sanna thinks, maybe rage is better than despair.

"Parker," a woman calls from behind them. They turn around.

It's Hadassah. "Wait for me," she calls and breaks into a little trot. Her short gray hair sticks up in the wind as she jogs toward them.

"I didn't know you'd be here," Parker says, confused.

"There's a counter demonstration against the ONEsters," Hadassah explains.

"Oh," Parker says. "Did you know about this?" she asks Nick, who shakes his head.

They walk together and the chants get louder as they get closer to the facility. Soon they can see the people chanting, white faces turned red with exhilaration, and holding signs with the American flag and the number 1.

Sanna looks at Hadassah who looks a bit pale. "Do you know anyone else coming to this?" she asks her. She doesn't want Hadassah to be alone while they go in to see her mom.

"Yes," Hadassah says. "But even if I'm the only one, my feet will be praying."

Sanna knows this reference. It comes from Rabbi Heschel, who marched with Martin Luther King, Jr., at Selma. Tembe told her about things like this as bedtime stories from the time she was a little girl. She can see why her mom would have called someone like Hadassah now, and she takes her hand to show her this.

"I'm glad you're here," Sanna says.

"Why, thank you, Sanna. I am, too." Hadassah gives Sanna's hand an affectionate squeeze.

They have to move through the crowd of ONEsters to get anywhere they want to go. Of course, Sanna and Nick and Parker want to go to the visitation area, but they are hesitant to leave Hadassah alone, so they go with her to look for the counter protesters.

"Jews won't replace us!" shouts a white man as they pass him, and it shakes Sanna to her bones. She thinks of Spearfinger, her calls in the night as she hunts for children, and wonders how anyone can listen to stuff like this, especially anyone Jewish, and not be afraid.

Hadassah still has her hand and squeezes it once, twice, and then smiles at her.

Hadassah is actually trying to comfort her while hearing this, Sanna realizes.

And then there they are. The counter protestors.

Behind a police barrier, just flimsy wooden things about waist high, a small group waits quietly.

Sanna can see Cecie there. And maybe three dozen other people, mostly women and people of color. They are not shouting. They are wearing all black. A few are holding signs with #resist or We Are All Immigrants on them.

They duck under the barriers and head toward Cecie. She hugs each of them.

"What's the circle for?" Sanna asks, pointing to Cecie's sign.

"It's a zero," she says. "They hold signs with a one. For the ONE policy. I made one with a zero because everything holds the possibility for dialogue when turned into a binary code."

"Sweet," says Nick, obviously impressed.

"It's visitation day," Cecie says, mostly to Parker. "I'm sure you can't wait to see her."

Parker's eyes fill with tears and Cecie hugs her. "It's gonna be okay," Cecie says, still holding her sign gingerly behind Parker.

"Hey, y'all," says Eden suddenly from behind them.

Sanna turns around. Asher is not there. Good. She wouldn't want it to slip that they went there the night before.

"Eden," Sanna says, taking the lead to cover up their deception. "This is my brother, Nick." And they shake hands.

"Do you know everyone?" Sanna asks, and they all nod. There are no hugs, though. A roar is going up through the ONEsters suddenly, and they all turn to face the crowd.

The inmates have been released into an area between the demonstrations and the building. They can't see them, but the noise and rage from the crowd lets them know what is happening.

My mom is in there somewhere, Sanna thinks. It is my mom they are screaming at. It is my mom who is bearing this screaming.

5.

Tembe lines up with the other students/inmates near a door that opens into the eastern yard.

"Citizens in training are not to engage with anyone outside the fence," one of the teacher/guards says, as the student/inmates go through the door. "Take a seat at one of the picnic tables," she says. "Spread out so everyone can have some privacy. And keep your back to the fence."

Tembe watches the crowd furtively as she makes her way quickly to a wooden picnic table, not wanting to end up with one too near the shouting horde. She is about to sit when she sees another woman grabbing the table and looking up defensively, so she moves to the next one.

It is hard to sit with her back to the fence. She would rather face them. She would rather see what is coming. Was this rule a way of protecting them from their hatred? Or a sly way of making them even more nervous?

And then they wait.

Waiting can be a quiet thing, Tembe thinks, remembering working in her studio at night, all the other faculty having gone home, her family asleep at home, too, and the silence a companion as she waited for the next spark of an idea on the canvas.

But this is the opposite of that. This is destruction and pressure and a kind of wide awake alertness as the morning turns toward noon and the sun bears down upon them on the warmer than normal November day.

Tembe sees Parker and Sanna and Nick coming out of the detention center, and for a second she is confused.

But of course they would have entered through the building so they could go through the metal detectors.

And this was why they are sitting facing the building, so they can see them entering and wave to them.

Tembe waves.

She waves to her wife, the person in her life that has calmed every worry Tembe brought to the marriage, some so old she didn't even remember they were there and certainly had never said out loud until Parker held her in her arms and said, "There, there," and Tembe let out the words in torrents of tears.

She waves to her daughter, the dark-haired miniature version of herself who is Tembe's greatest lesson in creation, as Sanna reminds her daily with her difference that no matter what you create with your hands or your body, no matter how much you love it and how much work you put into it, it is not you but its own separate, holy being.

She waves to Nick, the loping, gangly man he's becoming and the scared, small boy he was when she first met him, when Parker was still with his father and Parker and the boy both bore the visible scars of the man's hands upon them.

She waves to them. Her family. They walk to her. And even here, with the crowds chanting hate behind her and the gates locking them in and the teacher/guards tapping their weapons for good measure, even here, because they are here, she is home.

6.

"Mom," Sanna cries and falls into her mother's arms. Her mother is still taller than she is, but she won't be for much longer, at the rate Sanna is growing, but as Tembe holds her, Sanna wishes to be little again. Little enough to sit in her mom's lap the whole time they are there.

"Chickadee," her mom whispers and kisses the top of her head. Sanna loves it when her mom calls her that.

Nick is next. They don't talk, just hug, strong and quick, a wordless recognition that her mom is proud of him for being strong for Parker.

And then Parker. Sanna and Nick sit down at the picnic table as they stay standing and kiss each other long and hard on the lips, and Sanna can hear curses from the crowd beyond the fence.

She knows her moms don't care. What do they have to be afraid of, behind this fence, penned in already? What more punishment can they endure for being who they are?

Finally, they sit down. Parker and Sanna are on either side of Tembe, and Nick sits across from her. He is also the one to start talking.

"How long did they say you would be here?" he asks.

"Six months," Tembe says. There is a flatness to her voice.

"That's what we heard, too," Parker says. "As long as there's not an APA infraction."

"Yes," Tembe says, and turns to Parker. "Have you talked to Hadassah?"

Halloween night returns for all of them with the question.

"I did," says Parker.

"I did, too," Sanna offers.

"What?" Tembe asks, her eyes wide.

"I said no, I told her not to, but she went anyway," says Parker.

"You told her about the art?" Tembe snaps at Parker.

Parker opens her mouth, but nothing comes out. "I didn't. I only told her that Hadassah had called because you called her. You did call her."

Tembe looks down.

"She went to see Hadassah on her own, without my knowledge. She skipped school. And Hadassah was the one to tell her about the art."

Tembe looks up and turns to Sanna.

"What did you think?" she asks.

"She wouldn't let me see it," says Sanna.

Tembe is surprised. Her eyebrows shoot up and she grins. "Really? After ditching school and going rogue? She still wouldn't let you see it? That's hard core."

"That's what I thought, too."

"Hadassah is a bad ass," Tembe says. "That's why I called her. It's probably best you didn't see it. There's elements in the art that could be taken as subversive. Especially now."

They wait for her to say more.

She opens her mouth to speak but instead a deafening siren blares from the speakers in the yard.

7.

"Attention all citizens in training and guests," the voice bellows in between the sounds of the warning horn. "This is not a drill. The facility … the school … is on lockdown. Return to your bunks. I repeat. This is not a drill. All guests of the citizens in training must leave directly."

Tembe stands up, and Parker and Sanna and Nick look to her as if she's in charge.

"What's happening, Mom?" Sanna asks her.

"I don't know," Tembe says. "But you better go. Come on. Let's head in together."

"I was afraid of something like this," Nick says, and Tembe wonders what he means.

Parker is holding Tembe's hand so tightly it's going numb. They crush into the other inmate/students and their visitors as the crowd outside the gates seems to grow stronger, almost egged on by the blaring sirens and the sudden confusion.

Once inside, guard/teachers are directing them into two routes. To the right, further into the facility, everyone in uniform. To the left, out the door, everyone in street clothes.

"I love you," Parker yells as the crowd presses against them.

"I love you," Tembe says. "I love you, Sanna," she says, as she holds her hand out to touch her daughter one last time, but she can't reach her. Nick is taller, so she can see him just a beat longer than the others, and he puts his fist up in a black power sign toward her. She begins to raise her hand but thinks better of it at the last second, and suddenly she is down a hallway and, although the sirens are still blaring, at least the roar of the crowd is muffled, and Tembe feels something like relief as she flops onto her bunk.

8.

"But I don't want to go," Sanna is practically yelling at Parker as they make their way back through the crowd. What little is left of the group of counter protestors is also dispersing. Sanna can see a couple of them in their black outfits, their signs down by their sides, as they are heading to their cars.

"Sanna," Parker snaps at her. "Don't be stupid. This is a dangerous situation and there's no reason to stay. Your mom is in lockdown. For her own protection."

"But what's happening?" Sanna asks.

"I don't know. But we need to leave," Parker says.

Nick is saying nothing, following Parker and keeping his head down.

Parker walks more quickly, the bag of uneaten sandwiches bouncing against her hip as Sanna and Nick struggle to keep up. Cars are pulling out. All of a sudden, Parker stops, turns around.

"Wait," she says.

"For what?" Nick says. Sanna can hear the fear in his voice.

"Maybe Sanna is right. Maybe we shouldn't go. Maybe we can let this all die down and we can see Tembe some more."

"Mom," Nick pleads. "We should go."

Sanna wonders what he knows, and it makes her dizzy, remembering what he may have been trying to tell her this morning before she got in the shower. How she hushed him. How she didn't want to hear what he had to say.

Parker stands there in the middle of the gravel road, dust around her as cars drive past. Her eyes are bright like a deer in headlights. She is frozen.

She is trying to decide between her two children, Sanna knows, and between the sides of herself at war with each other. An impossible choice. Especially without Tembe there to help her.

Sanna decides to make the decision for her.

"Nick's right, Mom," Sanna says. "We should go. It's not ..." She is starting to say that it's not safe. She doesn't know what's happening, but she can tell from Nick's face that whatever it is, it is not safe. And then she realizes that saying so would make Parker want to stay. Out of concern for Tembe.

"It's not possible to see Mom any more today," Sanna says definitively, as if she's just been given this information from a reliable authority. "It's not going to happen. We should go."

Nick sighs and pats her shoulder, thankful for the help. "I'll drive, Mom," he says, and Parker hands him the keys.

As he starts the engine, the radio comes on with breaking news. No one dares to turn it off. Another mass shooting. This time in Wyoming. At a church. At least twenty presumed dead. They are waiting for authorities to release more information.

9.

The alarm stops blaring. It is deafeningly quiet. The afternoon sun comes through the barred window of her cell, but Tembe realizes suddenly that the lights on the ceiling are not on as usual.

She can still hear the echoes of the alarm in her head, but that's all she hears. She realizes that even the crowds outside have gone quiet.

How is that possible, so suddenly?

And then she smells smoke. Not just smoke. Something acrid. Chemical.

She sits up in her bunk.

Her bunkmate jumps down from the top bunk.

"What is happening?" Tembe can see Maggie's lips moving but can't hear her words.

There is a tinge in the air, and it is higher near the ceiling, Tembe notices as she stands up. Her visual senses are on alert, everything brighter and more vivid than normal. Like when she's painting. Like when she needs to make an escape.

But why can't she hear anything?

And then a wall of fire bursts into their cell.

10.

"Turn it off," says Parker wearily, pointing to the radio, her face pale and leaning against the passenger side window as they head onto the entrance ramp of the highway. "I can't take any more news. Every week it seems there's another terrorist attack, another mass shooting. This country's going to hell."

Nick switches off the radio and glances back at Sanna in the rearview mirror.

Parker's words echo in his eyes. This country's going to hell. That's what the ONEsters think, too. That's what Asher thinks, and Eden. Is it what Nick thinks?

Sanna closes her eyes. She sees Cecie's sign in her mind. The zero. The circle that creates the possibility of a dialogue with the 1.

Maybe it is possible for someone to go so far around a circle that they end up on the other side, Sanna thinks.

And then she doesn't want to think any more.

Parker is crying quietly in the front seat next to Nick. Nick is driving carefully, but quickly. He wants to get home to get more of the news, Sanna knows. Staying informed is his way of trying to make sense of everything. It was Parker's and Tembe's, too. Before Tembe was detained.

Sanna sits forward and puts her hand on Parker's shoulder. "It's gonna be okay," she says, and Parker tries to smile.

Sanna sits back and starts to put her earbuds in, but Parker's phone rings and Sanna waits.

"Hello?" Parker says. "Cecie?"

Nick and Sanna look at each other.

"Yes, we're heading home."

"Okay. But are you sure it's safe?"

"Okay, then."

Parker hangs up. "Cecie is meeting us at the house," she says.

"But Mom?" Nick asks. "What about the APA?"

"I'm tired, Nick," Parker says, crying. "I'm so tired of living in fear. It's only been a few days since she's been gone, I know, but it feels so much longer. I miss her so much, and if her friends want to come over, well, then, I'm going to let them come over."

His fingers head toward the radio dial. "Shouldn't we find out what's happening?" he asks.

"No," she says. "I don't want to hear it from a stranger."

Sanna doesn't know what she means by this but she feels a cold sharpness in her belly, as if Spearfinger has poked her there. She puts the earbuds and her phone down. Face down. She doesn't want to see any notifications. She does not know what is happening, and she doesn't want to know.

Nick steps on the gas and drives over the speed limit.

Parker's eyes are closed and she says nothing.

Sanna looks out the window at the trees along the side of the highway, glowing in their fall colors under bright sunshine, and thinks about how, even now, her mother would say it's a beautiful day.

11.

Cecie is waiting on their front porch when they arrive home. She is sitting next to their two pumpkins, no longer bearing the faces of Jack O'lanterns but crushed in from humidity and looking like gaping mouths.

"Parker," Cecie says, standing. "I'm so glad you all made it out all right."

"What's happening?" Nick says.

"Everyone let's just go inside first," says Parker, taking the keys from Nick and opening the front door. The scent of the pancakes from the morning still lingers in the air as they step into the house.

"Do you want tea?" asks Parker.

"Mom," says Nick. "Why is Cecie here?"

"I'm sure she didn't want to be alone," says Parker. "It was quite a hard day for everyone."

Sanna looks at Cecie. She looks like a cat who's dragged in a mouse. There's something she's not saying, Sanna can tell.

Sanna walks to her and looks into her deep gray eyes.

"Is it my mother?" Sanna asks.

"Can we sit down?" Cecie answers.

Sanna's stomach hurts and she almost bends at the waist from the pain as she sits on the couch. Cecie sits next to her. Parker and Nick huddle on the love seat across from them.

Cecie looks out the window. Then speaks. "After you went in to the detention facility, Eden told me to leave."

"Why?" Nick asks. "What did she know?"

Cecie's eyes flash at Nick. "I wasn't sure," she says. "But she said it wasn't safe. She said The ReSisters heard a rumor."

"Is that why the alarm went off?" Nick asks.

"I don't know," Cecie says. "But I decided to leave. Eden seemed pretty shaken. I didn't want to take any chances."

"Did it have something to do with the shooting in Wyoming?" Nick asks.

"I don't know," says Cecie. "They are not reporting that there's a connection."

"Connection?" Parker asks, her voice shaking. "What connection?"

"Between the two events," says Cecie.

"Events?" says Sanna, and her stomach is really hurting now.

"The shooting in Wyoming and the explosion at the detention center."

"Explosion?" cries Parker.

"You haven't heard?" Cecie asks.

"Damn it, Mom!" Nick says. "You made us turn off the radio!" He leaves the room and they can hear his laptop chiming on.

"Cecie," Parker almost whispers. "What happened?"

Cecie speaks quietly. "There was an explosion in the facility. It seems some of the ONEsters were able to get into the building with the visitors, and they set the alarm off so the place could go on lockdown. Once the lockdown was in place, a bomb went off."

Sanna cannot believe her voice still works, but she has to know the answer.

"Was anyone hurt?" she asks.

Cecie reaches out and takes Sanna's hand. "Oh, my dear," she says. "Yes."

"No!" Parker cries, and Cecie stands up to go to her. Sanna watches as Cecie holds her while she sobs.

"Not my mom," she whispers, a prayer, a supplication, a request. To God. To whoever is listening.

And, like Rabbi Heschel, her feet continue to pray as she gets up and walks out of the room toward Nick's room to get more information.

Nick is at his desk and has the computer screen open to 8space.

"What happened?" she says, sitting on his bed, tears streaming down her face.

He looks over at her. "They don't know for sure. They think the ONEsters breached the facility and planted a bomb."

"Cecie said there are injuries."

"They are claiming hundreds are dead."

"Who is claiming that?"

"The ONEsters," Nick says. "They released a statement that said 'Eradication not education.'"

Sanna crumples onto his unmade bed. It smells of boy. It smells of sleepless nights and worry. She starts to sob, and he comes over to her, gestures for her to slide over, and sits down next to her, rubbing her back.

"Squirta," he says so quietly she can almost not hear him. "I'm so sorry."

12.

Parker's phone rings. They can hear it from Nick's room but they can't hear what she is saying, so they go back to the living room.

"Yes?" Parker says, and waits. "Okay," she says. "Thank you. I'll be right there."

Parker looks up. "It was Dixon. He says they've set up a center for families to be notified."

"Where?" Nick asks.

"At a church near the …" Parker doesn't finish the sentence, bursts into tears.

"I don't want to go," says Sanna. She cannot imagine being around strangers, being comforted by strangers, hearing any news from strangers. She wants to crawl into her bed and never wake up.

"We can't let my mom go alone," Nick says.

"I'll go with her," Cecie offers.

Parker looks up. "No," she says. "We can't leave the kids alone. There should be an adult here."

"I'll stay with them then," says Cecie.

"No," says Nick. "I want to be with my mom. You stay with Sanna."

Cecie looks to Parker to make the decision. "I'll do whatever you need," she says.

"I think I'd like Nicky to be with me," Parker says. "And you, too, Sanna. But you can stay if you want." She looks over at Sanna, who can't look at her. Her grief is too great.

"I just can't go," says Sanna. "I just need to be home."

"Okay," says Cecie. "I'll stay then."

Sanna goes to her room and closes the door. Her bed is made. She hardly ever makes her bed, but she did that morning. Because she was going to see her mom. Because she wanted her to be proud of her. Even if she wasn't there.

The thought of it causes her to crumple down on the neatly made bed, sobbing.

She doesn't hear as Parker and Nick leave. She doesn't hear Cecie making the tea that was offered but never made. She hears nothing but the sound of her own voice saying over and over, "Mama. Mama."

She doesn't sleep. She loses track of the hours and soon it is nightfall, too soon as it always is on the day the clocks fall back. As if time itself has fallen back with grief.

She doesn't hear a sound from the rest of the house. Maybe Cecie left, she thinks, and she ventures out of her dark room quietly.

"Sanna," Cecie says softly from a chair in the living room. There is a small lamp lit on the table beside her, and an empty tea cup next to it. She holds a book in her lap. "Are you hungry? I could make dinner."

"No, thanks," Sanna says. "Have you heard anything?"

"They haven't called. And I haven't turned on the news."

"Okay."

"When was the last time you ate?" Cecie asks.

"Breakfast," Sanna says. "But I'm not hungry."

"Okay. I understand," Cecie says. "But is there anything I can do for you?"

Sanna thinks. Bring my mom back?

She shakes her head. But then she has an idea.

"Actually, you know what would be good?" she asks.

"What? Anything."

"I could really use a milkshake. My stomach has been hurting, and my mom gets me a mint milkshake from that place on Route 27 when my stomach hurts after school."

Cecie smiles. "You got it. Let's go."

"Um, could you go? Do you mind? I just can't."

Cecie hesitates for a second, and then picks up her purse. "Sure. I'll be right back. Mint milkshake coming up. Anything else?"

"No. Thank you."

When Cecie's car has pulled away, Sanna goes into Nick's room. Clicks on the keyboard to light up the computer. There it is. She sees the headlines about the day's events on the top of the screen.

Sanna takes the laptop to her room and settles in to try to find out more about what is happening.

This is not news, though. 8space is filled with diatribes against immigrants, theories about the Wyoming shooting being tied to Muslim terrorism, congratulations for the deaths of inmates at the ONE facility who had it coming.

When she can't take anymore, she clicks away and tries something else.

What she reads, even on the legitimate news sites, are thousands of comments about the day's events, mostly skewed toward the ONEsters and filled with hate. Not as boldfaced as the language on 8space and mostly coded in terms Sanna doesn't understand, but it's the same. Hate. Damnation.

She thinks back to Parker's statement in the car. "This country is going to hell."

Maybe we are already there, thinks Sanna.

She hears a car in the driveway. For a second she allows herself to hope. Parker and Nick are home? Already?

She rushes to replace the laptop in Nick's room and goes to the front door.

It's Cecie. With her milkshake and tears in her eyes.

13.

"Oh, sugar," Cecie says and wraps Sanna in her arms.

"What? What is it?" Sanna's mouth is forming the words but she doesn't really want to hear the answer. She is dizzy with anticipation. Dread.

"Let's sit down," Cecie says. She looks as if she might fall down herself.

She puts the milkshake on the coffee table, puts her purse by her feet, and takes both of Sanna's hands in hers.

"Your mama," she says, and then stops.

Sanna feels the knives in her belly, the ones that have been cutting her all day, begin to twist and heat as if they are becoming red hot pokers.

She doesn't move. She doesn't say anything.

"I'm so sorry, baby," Cecie says, crying. "Your mama called me when I was coming back from the ice cream shop."

"My mom?" Sanna asks.

"Parker," Cecie says.

Sanna remembers something she read on one of the threads on Nick's laptop. It was an invective against homosexuals, calling them "it" and saying that even the newfangled "they" and "them" was not enough for those who did not like men to be men and women to be women. "Them" was still a word that meant human, it said. "They" was a word that said they were still people. But these were abominations against the nation. Its.

Her mother.

Her mothers.

"What did she say?"

"She said they posted lists of the survivors at the center. Honey, I'm so sorry, but your mom's name wasn't on it."

It. Her mother was an "it" they killed. Her other mother was an "it" who called.

When they killed her mother, they did not commit one murder but the murder of a family.

An eye for an eye.

A life for a life.

Sanna takes one of her hands from Cecie and reaches toward the coffee table very slowly and deliberately.

Cecie watches her carefully.

Sanna picks up the milkshake and brings the bright red straw to her lips. Takes a sip. The thick green liquid makes its way through the tube and onto her tongue.

Cold. So cold it is almost painful as she swallows once, twice, three times, feeling the ice numbing her gums and the back of her throat.

Allowing the frozen feeling to seep into her head and chest and belly.

Putting out the fires that have been bellowing and flaming there all day.

Longer, actually.

Since she heard her mother was gone. Since she knew, at some level, that her mother would never come home, despite Sanna's best intentions and making her bed that morning and asking everyone she could think of for some advice, some kind of wisdom, to stop this from happening.

There is no one.

No one can help her now.

Because as she drinks the milkshake, swallow after swallow, with Cecie's wide, gray eyes watching, Sanna is hatching a plan.

The world will end in fire or ice, she learned from some poem in English class. And Sanna has had quite enough of fire.

She is ready for ice.

14.

Sanna wakes on Monday morning after a night of vivid dreams to a morning filled with fog. The fog feels like it's inside her, too, as if yesterday might have been a part of a bad dream. She knows it is not, though.

She hears the television on in the living room and wonders what time it is. Is Cecie still there? Did Parker and Nick ever come home?

She soon finds Parker in front of the television. Her face is a map of worry lines.

"Sanna," says Parker, and holds her hands up. "Come here to me."

Sanna goes to her, lets herself be hugged. But there is something weird in how Parker is acting.

"It was domestic violence again, can you believe that?" Parker says.

"What?" Sanna says.

"That shooting in Wyoming."

"Oh." Sanna cannot believe that this is what Parker is choosing to focus on. Today.

"When did you get home?" Sanna asks, trying to draw her attention away from the distraction of the news.

"Around midnight. The people at the center were very nice. It's going to be a couple days before ...."

"Before what?"

"Before the ashes are ready. We have to plan a memorial. I'm waiting 'til the funeral parlor opens at ten to call."

Sanna looks into Parker's eyes and sees she's not really there.

"Where's Nick?" Sanna asks.

"He went to school. He had a test."

"Oh." Sanna tries to bring Parker's mothering out from under the blanket of fog she's obviously in. "What about me? Don't you think I should go to school, too?"

Parker waves her hand. "Oh, Sanna," she says. "I figured I'd leave it up to you."

Sanna shakes her head. Is it possible that she lost two mothers in one day?

Parker's eyes go back to the television once the commercial is over.

Sanna gets up and walks away. Goes back into her room and sits on her unmade bed.

Images flash in front of her, bringing strangely stinging temporary relief from the fog sitting all around.

Tembe's face as she begins to raise her fist toward Nick in the detention center and then is led away.

Nick telling her the ONEsters released a statement saying "Eradication not education."

The circle on Cecie's sign.

Pixelated letters shaping words of hate on Nick's computer screen.

The red straw in her milkshake.

Hadassah's hand in hers as they walk through the crowd yelling about the Jews.

There's only one thing she wants to do.

And the first step is to call Hadassah.

15.

Sanna's room has an eerie glow from the fog outside the window as she digs through her backpack on her bed.

She takes out lip gloss and pencils, a date book and a late slip, before finding it.

Hadassah's number, scribbled while Parker was in the shower that day when Sanna decided to skip school and go see her. It feels like a repetition, not letting Parker know and reaching out to Hadassah on a school day.

But it's not.

Nothing, even if she did it exactly the same, would be the same as it was, ever again. It is as if Sanna is two people now. There was her life before, the Sanna she was when she had a mother, and life, if it can even be called that, now.

Without a mother.

She closes her door quietly, picks up her phone, and dials.

No need for secrecy now. No need to hide anything. There is no Tembe to protect, nothing she needs to fear.

"Hello?" Hadassah answers.

"Hadassah. It's Sanna."

"Sanna, dear. I am so sorry about your mother."

"Thank you." Sanna pauses, then says it. "Hadassah, I was wondering if it would be okay now to see my mom's art."

She can hear Hadassah take a sharp breath.

"I'm not teaching today," Hadassah says. "I'm home. Would you like to come over?"

"Yes, please."

Sanna writes down the address on the same crumpled paper where the number is written, and then, after hanging up, transfers both to her phone.

There is nothing to fear any more.

Parker barely looks at her as Sanna says she's going out. No sage has been burned at dawn today. No poetry notebook rests in her lap. No cheerful breakfast has been made.

And Sanna catches a whiff of the scent of red wine coming from the coffee mug that Parker clutches in both hands as she stares at the television screen.

Hadassah lives near the campus and Sanna has no choice but to walk. Tembe was going to start teaching her to drive when she got back from the Netherlands, Sanna suddenly remembers, and then pushes the thought away.

Half of the red leaves from the dogwood tree are in a circle on the ground as Sanna crosses the front yard. The fog lingers even though the temperature is rising steadily on a Monday morning. Her street is quiet. As she walks, it seems the whole town is quiet. It is hard to believe that this is the same world where so many awful things are happening.

That makes it almost worse for Sanna. The incongruence of this.

She wishes that bombs were falling.

She wishes that so many people were dying that no one could deny what is happening.

Something to show her she is not alone in this.

Hadassah's house is a cute one-story cottage. Instead of a lawn, she has a garden of rocks and plants and a curving stone pathway to the front door.

She opens the door quickly after Sanna knocks, and she is wearing all black. For a second, Sanna wonders if she even changed her clothes since yesterday, but then remembers that Hadassah was wearing black slacks and a top then, and now she's in a long dress.

As she steps inside, she recalls the newscaster mentioning the Wyoming shooter in all-black, too, and it occurs to her that even color itself has ceased to signify something specific. It could be resistance or mourning or hate or anything in between.

"Come out back," Hadassah says. "It's turning into quite a nice day. I've made some rugelach and I have tea for us out there."

Sanna isn't sure what that is but she heads through the house to double French doors, opened in the back to a wonderful little garden. There is a koi pond and stone statues. Sanna can see figures of a turtle and a rabbit and the Buddha and a woman that her mother told her stories about but can't remember her name.

"What is her name again?" she asks Hadassah, pointing to the statue of the woman near the pond.

"Kwan Yin. Goddess of Compassion."

"Right." Sanna almost smiles. "My mom told me her father was cruel to her and she went to live on an island all by herself. That sounds pretty good right now."

Hadassah smiles and nods. "Yes, I'm sure it does. Did your mom also tell you what she does on that island?"

Sanna thinks for a second and nods. "Prays for everyone with compassion."

"That's right."

"That may be more than I can handle doing," Sanna says.

"That's why she does it," says Hadassah. "Because sometimes we can't do it ourselves. Because sometimes we need her to."

They sit down at a small table with chairs covered in brightly colored cushions. A flowered ceramic pot of tea is on the table with two matching cups. And a plate of what looks like croissants with some kind of dark filling.

"What is that again?" Sanna asks. She hopes she doesn't sound rude.

"Rugelach. A Jewish pastry. I make mine with pecans. Because we're in the south. Want to try it?"

"Yes, please."

Hadassah serves two on a plate and puts it in front of Sanna, then gets two for herself and pours cups of tea for them both.

"Amaretto tea," she says. "To match the nutty flavor."

Sanna takes a bite. The filling is like pecan pie, but not quite as sweet. The crust is like a croissant, but not as flaky. Almost like a bread.

"It's good," she says. "Thank you." She realizes she hardly ate at all the day before.

"You're welcome." Hadassah takes a big bite of hers. "Not bad if I do say so myself."

They eat and sip quietly for a while. A cardinal comes to the birdfeeder, chirps, and watches them.

"My mom called that a redbird," Sanna says quietly. And this is the first sentence she utters since learning of her mother's death that is not foggy with numbness, tinged with the sharp sword of anger, or swallowed in a well of grief.

"Your mom taught you so very much," Hadassah says gently.

And Sanna nods. Waits. She feels more patient around Hadassah. As if time is more generous.

The wind shifts slightly and all of a sudden the fog is gone and it is a sunny day.

Hadassah finishes her second rugelach, wipes her hands on a cloth napkin, and then reaches into her pocket.

"Give me your hand," she says.

And Sanna holds out her palm.

Hadassah places a computer flash drive into it, folds her fingers over Sanna's, and says, "There you go."

"What is it?"

"Your mother's book."

"I thought it was art."

"It is. When I heard the news about your mother last night, I stayed up late scanning it at the office. I thought you might call. And I figured this way you could keep it with you more easily."

Sanna can't see it, only feel the plastic in her palm, and is a bit disappointed. She had wanted something her mother had created with her own hands.

"Where is the actual book?" Sanna asks.

"Still hidden. Safe."

"You still think it needs to be kept safe?"

"Always."

Sanna remembers her manners and thanks Hadassah. "It was nice of you to think of me, to do this for me," she says.

"You are welcome."

Some orange leaves fall toward the southeast in the breeze. It looks like they are flying.

"There's something else," Hadassah says.

"Yes?"

"Your mother told me you don't have a computer of your own. She said you use the one from school but that she was planning to give you one for Christmas."

Sanna didn't know this.

"So, I don't think it's a good idea for you to use the school computer for this."

Sanna thinks about the slim chance of borrowing Nick's computer for very long.

"It's not a computer, but it works very well, especially for visual art," Hadassah says, as she pulls a box from under the table.

It's a brand new tablet.

"Oh, my goodness," Sanna says. She feels stupid, like a little kid, that something like this could make her so happy. But it does. "Thank you!"

"You are welcome. I had to get it at Wal-mart. Don't tell anyone. Nothing else was open late on a Sunday night. It was an emergency."

Sanna smiles at her, and they sit quietly. Sanna holds the box in one hand and the flash drive in the other.

"Well, aren't you going to open it?" Hadassah asks.

"Now?" Sanna asks.

"No time like the present." She smiles. She stands and begins picking up the plates and then stops. Puts her hand in her pocket and says, "Oh, I almost forgot. You'll need this, too. The woman at the store says it connects the flash drive to the tablet. Not that I understand what that really means."

Sanna reaches up for the small white box and says, "Thank you so much."

Hadassah continues clearing the table and says, "I have some grading to do. Combine that with the fact that I didn't get very much sleep last night, and I foresee a nap on my agenda. Stay as long as you like. Make more tea. Get yourself something to eat. Whatever you want."

Sanna cannot believe how generous she is being. "Thank you so much," she says, and as she does, she realizes how little she actually wants to return home. Especially when Parker is dealing with all of this in such a weird way.

"I think I will stay a while," Sanna says.

Just then an orange marmalade cat slinks up to Sanna's chair.

"Oh, there you are, Winston," Hadassah says. "Been out all night again, you bad cat?"

"I didn't know you had a cat," Sanna says. "I love cats! My brother is allergic."

"He's a very British, very snooty, very bad boy," says Hadassah, with love in her voice. "He probably heard the word 'nap' and came running."

Sanna pets him as he purrs loudly by her leg.

Hadassah smiles. "Or maybe he heard you were staying."

Sanna goes over to a lounge chair under a maple tree near the koi pond, and Winston, to her great delight, follows her. She sits down on the chair and opens the box.

She is just about to ask Hadassah for her wi-fi password when Hadassah says from just inside the French doors, "I wrote the wi-fi password on the box. You may need to do some research to read the book."

"Your mom is a very smart and very nice woman, did you know that, Winston?" Sanna asks the cat. He circles and then settles at the end of the lounge chair between her feet as she sets up the tablet.

"My mom was, too, actually," she says to him, quietly and sadly, opening the file containing her mother's book.

Part Three

SITA

Circle
is
a
word and a
shape and a
sound
and yet
silent
until you
say it but
can't you
make
it.

1.

"What the …," Sanna says out loud, looking at the first page of her mother's book as it opens on her new tablet. This doesn't make any sense.

But of course.

That's exactly what it says.

"I can't make it," Sanna says out loud. "I don't understand."

She thinks back to the icy thought she had the night before, gulping the mint milkshake, deliberating something that had never even come close to crossing her mind before. And Cecie's circle. The zero. Or a circle?

She looks again at the letters at the top of the page. And then it hits her. It's Cherokee.

Could the word mean circle?

Grateful for wi-fi, Sanna types "Cherokee circle" into the browser and learns Sammy Hagar and The Circle are performing at the Harrah's in Cherokee that Thursday.

Jackpot, she chuckles to herself as she remembers her mother talking about the controversies over gambling and drinking at the Harrah's in Cherokee. She doesn't think that's what her mom means, though.

She tries something else. "Cherokee word for circle."

After a few failed attempts—everyone has these when they gamble, she tells herself— she finds a Cherokee Dikaneisdi. Not exactly a dictionary, more of a word list search engine that allows her to put in words in Cherokee or English and get the translation.

Working backwards, Sanna types in the word for "circle" and there it is. The Cherokee word that is the first word of her mother's book.

She clicks the audio button and hears "Gawsahquayla." In the list, it is written as "ga-so-qua-lv."

She repeats it to herself a few times in her head, then tries it on her tongue.

"Gasoqualv," she says out loud in a clear voice. "See, Mom? I can make it."

Something in her comes full circle as she runs her finger across the screen of the tablet to turn to the next page.

Warrior
is
a word
that combines
war

ᏔᎦᏪᎠᏓᎵᎠ

danuga
and
anihali
Sometimes spelled
inali
which means
Black Fox
who was
a
Cherokee Chief

and it all
comes
back to the
chief.

2.

"How's it going?"

Sanna jumps at the sound of Hadassah's voice. She looks down at the document and notices the time. Almost two hours have passed. How did that happen?

"Uh, good, I guess," says Sanna.

"I guess you can see why I gave you the tablet," Hadassah says. "It's not a usual book. I thought you might need the help with researching while reading it."

"Yes," says Sanna, and all of a sudden, she's starving. She doesn't want to impose on Hadassah any more, though, so she says, "I think I better get going. Parker will wonder where I am." She's not sure this is true, but she says it anyway.

"You're welcome to stay," Hadassah says. "I can make lunch."

But suddenly Sanna wants to be back home, alone if that's possible. "Thank you so much for everything," she says. "I should go."

"Call me anytime," says Hadassah, showing her to the door.

Winston the cat follows them, rubbing Sanna's calves as they hug goodbye.

"Winston says you can come back anytime. You know you are always welcome."

As Sanna walks down the street with the tablet in her backpack, she feels the weight of her mother upon her. The weight of history. It's heavy like the stone skin of Spearfinger. It's sharp like the knife of hunger in her belly.

And yet it's empty. Like the circles in her mother's book. Waiting to be filled up.

Her phone buzzes. It's Nick.

"There's a sub in chemistry. He's not taking attendance. Wanna meet for lunch?"

"Sure," she texts back. "Grump's?"

It's their favorite deli, and it's not far from Hadassah's house.

ᎤᏓᎵᎢ

is
pronounced
doyugodv

and means
justice
and
truth
and
right
and
honest
and
outright
and

English
has so many words
for something
that sounds like
"Do you, duh?"

3.

"What's that?" Nick comes up behind Sanna at the deli, his eyes wide as he looks at the new tablet.

Sanna is not sure she wants to tell him about the book. Yet. So she quickly closes the file and says, "Hadassah gave it to me."

"Why?"

"Can we order first?" she asks. "I'm starving."

"Okay," he says, and they line up at the counter. When they are asked if it's for there or to go, Sanna says, "Let's take it to the park."

While they wait for the order, Nick asks again, "Why did Hadassah give you an iPad?"

"Isn't that the wrong question?" she teases him.

"What do you mean?"

"You were the one who taught me to ask what instead of why."

"Sanna," he says. "Come on."

"Okay," she says, lowering her voice conspiratorially, "She gave it to me so I could read my mom's book."

"You got it?" he exclaims. "That's great!"

"Yeah, well. Maybe. It doesn't make much sense so far."

"What's it about?"

"Cherokee history? Language? Justice? I honestly don't know."

"You want some help?"

And she says yes. Actually, she would like very much to have his help with this.

Hurt and injury happen when the circle is broken and truth justice honesty and outright transparency are washed away.

O'RCA SĦIA

4.

Nick and Sanna are sitting at a picnic table at "their" park. It's just a small patch of grass with a swing set and a slide, but they've been coming there since they moved into the house, at first with their moms to play on the equipment, and then riding their bikes on their own, and later, when adolescence hit, using it as a place to lick their wounds when one of them didn't get their way with something.

They are older now. They haven't been here in years. But somehow it is fitting. It still feels like their park, especially now in the early afternoon, with younger kids home for their naps and older kids still in school.

They have inhaled their sandwiches as only teenagers can, and Sanna has shown the first few panels— she guesses this is the right word; they are not quite chapters and not quite paintings but something in between—of her mother's book to Nick.

"Whoa," he says. "Is all of this a book about the president?"

She thought so, too, but hadn't formulated it into a clear question yet. "Maybe?" she says.

"I can see why you'd want help with it, Squirta," he says. "I'll help you in any way I can."

And then he pauses, looks at his hands. They are a man's hands already, Sanna thinks, still remembering what he looked like when they first met.

"I need to talk to you about something," he says. "I wanted to meet for lunch because I didn't want to do it around Mom."

"She was pretty freaked out this morning," Sanna says.

"Yeah, that's what I meant. There's something I think it's time for you to know."

This scares her a little, but she says, "What is it?"

"My mom. Why she left my dad. Did anyone ever tell you that?"

"No."

"I think all this is triggering it for her. It was pretty bad." He pauses. "I don't know if this is the right time."

"Nick, you can't stop now. Just tell me."

"Okay. Here goes. It's been a long time since I said this out loud to anyone. The only time, actually, was during my parents' divorce. I had to go see this counselor."

He pauses. Sanna senses he might stop there.

"Please. I want to hear it," she says softly.

"Well, my dad, you know, the great and powerful senator from Oz? He's an abuser. He hit my mom and he hit me. A lot. There were times we couldn't even leave the house, we had so many bruises. Or things broken."

Sanna listens. Doesn't interrupt.

He holds up his left index finger. It is slightly bent backwards. She's never noticed it before. He tries to touch it to his thumb to make a circle and form the sign for "okay." He can't.

"The broken circle," she says quietly. "Like in my mom's book."

"Yeah. I was going to tell you anyway. When I saw how my mom was acting this morning. But then, just now, I knew. I don't know, maybe it's going to sound stupid. But it's like your mom wanted me to tell you now."

"You could be right," she says gently. "I think there's a lot my mom wants us to know." She can't bring herself to speak in the past tense.

"So, anyway, that's why I hardly ever see him. My dad. Ha. I don't even use that word very much. But I wanted to tell you about it so you could maybe understand what my mom's going through. I think that thing in Wyoming has really triggered her. She's kind of losing it, I think."

Sanna nods.

"I know my mom has never loved anyone as much as she loved your mom," he says.

He's using the past tense, Sanna notices.

"Me, too," he says. "I loved her very much. She was the best dad I ever had."

He smiles at the joke, but there are tears in his eyes.

Sanna's, too.

DWƏI alasdi or fight is not the same word we think of as fighting and is connected to the words for baseball football dancing economics and trampling. It means to use your feet.

5.

"Did you ever hear the story of the Ring Fight?" Nick asks her after they've dipped into the book again and seen that the next panel is about fighting.

The sun has made its way westward and the breeze picks up a bit as it does on a humid afternoon in the south.

"No. What's that?"

"My dad was obsessed with Revolutionary War history. He fancied himself some kind of descendant, I guess, because he was from Pennsylvania. Maybe that's why this story meant so much to him."

"What story?"

"The story of Andrew Pickens and The Ring Fight."

"Who is that? Some kind of boxer?"

He laughs. "No, not exactly. It's weird, talking about him today to you, it's like suddenly I'm remembering all these things I haven't thought about in years."

"Hey, Nick," Sanna says, yawning. "Do you still have your sleeping bag in the trunk? I'd love to stretch out while I hear this story. I didn't sleep very well last night."

"Sure, Squirta," and he pops the trunk on the Subaru. He goes to fetch it for her like a good big brother, and as he comes back, she's looking around, trying to choose a good tree to sit under for storytelling, like they used to do when they were younger.

She picks a sycamore. She has always liked the magic of the seedpod balls that they drop. He unrolls the sleeping bag like a blanket. He sits down and she curls up like a bunny next to him with her hands under her face.

"Tell me, oh, great brother," she teases, "the legend of the Ring Fight."

"Alrighty. So," he begins, "Andrew Pickens is not a learned man. I mean, you hear about Washington and Jefferson and Adams. They were upper class, you know? This Pickens, he was basically a redneck from rural Pennsylvania. Scotch-Irish descent."

"The lowest." Sanna grins, knowing he is also descended from this stock.

"And he makes his way down to Carolina where he becomes a military captain, basically in charge of slaughtering Cherokees."

"Your dad told you this story when you were a little kid? At bedtime?" Sanna asks.

Nick nods. "Nice guy, huh?"

"So one day," he continues, "Pickens is with this regiment of about twenty or thirty. They get word that there's a Cherokee village up ahead, and they think, well, we'll get them now, and they come in all quiet-like thinking it's going to be easy."

Sanna hopes she's guessing what happens next.

"And all of a sudden, this Indian warrior pops out of the grass, and then another and another. There are like two hundred of them. And the colonial forces are surrounded."

"Good," says Sanna.

"That's why it's called the Ring Fight. The Indians had them surrounded and outnumbered, and Pickens tells his men to form two concentric circles and get low to the ground."

"Concentric circles?" asks Sanna.

"Yeah. The one on the outside shoots while the one on the inside reloads. So they can keep going without pausing to reload."

"Without pausing to reload," she repeats, thinking of the many mass shootings recently, all done by white men.

"And even though they're surrounded, and even though they are outnumbered at least ten to one, and even though the Indians advance on them so thoroughly that it turns into a tomahawk fight and Pickens says at the end that every single one of them was covered with blood and smoke, they win."

"They win?"

"Yup. They defeated the Cherokee in the Ring Fight and scalped as many Indian corpses as they could. The Indians were slowed down because from time to time they paused in their fighting to drag their dead and injured away, not wanting the bodies desecrated like that."

"I thought Indians were the ones who did the scalping."

"That's what they tell you in the history books at school, isn't it?"

"Man," she says.

"Exactly." He nods and continues, "Pickens and his men also set fire to a sugar cane field nearby, and, as it burned, it popped like gunfire, leading the Indians to believe that reinforcements had come. Then they burned down the nearby village where they were headed in the first place, including all the corn and beans and livestock so the Indians lost not only their homes but all their food."

"That's horrible!"

"That's my dad for you. He considered that a bedtime story. And a good one. You want to know the weird thing?"

"What?"

"The Ring Fight took place in 1776. That's not what we remember about 1776, is it?"

"No."

They are quiet for a while, watching the kids who are out of school now playing on the playground equipment while their moms watch on benches nearby.

"Nick?"

"Yeah?"

"Did you tell me that story because my mom is … well, because she …." Sanna doesn't want to say it. She thinks about the Indian villages pillaged and razed in the year that the country was founded. She thinks about scalping dead Indian bodies. She thinks, even though she doesn't want to, of her mother's body. Did she suffer? Was she alone when it happened? Where were her wounds?

Sanna will never know.

So she stops. And opens the tablet again.

Body also means health and is connected to the words for nation capital taxes funds anarchy and diameter. It is all a circle.

DBa

111

6.

"No, Sanna," Nick says tenderly. "I didn't tell you that story for you. I told it for me. Because, well, the truth is I'm so angry."

Sanna's ears perk up when he says this, and she puts the tablet down and sits up. Can he be thinking along the same lines that she is? She knows he's seen the same internet threads and comments that she saw the other day, even more of them, really. She knows that he has also lost a mother like she has.

"Angry? At who? At your dad? Is that why you told me what happened when you were little?"

"Well, yeah, of course, I'm angry at him. But not really for what happened anymore. It's like numb, you know? It's just that it's coming up now for my mom. And, well, I mean, I'm mad at the whole nation, really. That's why your mom's book made me think of the Ring Fight. It's like everything was so messed up from the beginning."

"I'm mad, too," Sanna says, but she doesn't lift her eyes for fear he'll see the ice-cold rage she keeps inside.

"You want to know what's absolutely the most gnarly part of that story about Pickens? The thing my dad reveled in saying right before turning out the light and telling me goodnight?"

"What?"

"The thing is, the Cherokee came to respect Andrew Pickens after that battle. He went on and burned almost all of the villages in what was called the Lower Cherokee area, throughout South Carolina and Georgia and the foothills of North Carolina, and then they gave him the name of their beloved chief who was called The Wizard Owl. They revered his ferocity. They actually ended up liking the bastard."

"Sounds like a commander-in-chief we might know right now," Sanna ventures, but hesitantly, not wanting to say too much.

"Right? I mean, it's like how my dad is this great senator and everything now. People send money to him. I mean, Asher was right. The corporations basically have the politicians in their back pockets. They own them. But still there's an aura of respect. There's a belief that the politicians are in it for the right reasons. But I haven't really believed in it for a long time. Because my dad is an asshole. There's no other word for it."

He looks at his watch. "We better get home," he says. "We'd just be getting out of school right now if we'd gone to school, and I don't want Mom to worry."

"Wait one minute," Sanna says, grabbing his arm. "Do you really think there's nothing we can do about it?"

"My dad? The country? The president?"

"Any of it."

"No." He looks up at a kid squealing from the top of the slide. "Honestly, no. I'm thinking it's all kind of doomed. And I'm more worried about my mom right now."

"What can we do for her, Nick?"

"I don't know. I just wanted you to know what's behind all of this, all of her weirdness. I haven't even seen her cry about your mom yet. She's just obsessed with that shooting."

"I know."

They gather up the sleeping bag, put it back in the trunk, and get in the car.

"Let's see how she's doing when we get home," Sanna says. "I'll call Cecie if we need her."

7.

They hear the wailing even before they walk in the house.

"Oh, my God," Nick says, running toward the front door. "Is that my mom?"

Sanna thinks of the noise Spearfinger makes when she's on the hunt for children. She imagines it sounds like this. A long, low moan of a woman out of control.

When they get inside, Parker is crumpled up on the kitchen floor, sobbing. Her hair is wild and there are red wine stains on her shirt. Two empty wine bottles are on the counter.

"Mom, Mom," Nick urges her to look at him, kneeling beside her on the linoleum. "Look at me. I'm here. I'm here. It's okay. I'm here."

"It's not okay," Parker screams. "It's never going to be okay!"

"She's drunk," Sanna says, as if that will somehow help the situation.

"I can see that," Nick snaps at her. "Help me get her into bed, will you?"

Parker doesn't stop sobbing as they each take one side and lead her into the bedroom.

"It's going to be okay," Nick keeps repeating.

"Do you think we should call someone? Cecie maybe?" Sanna asks.

"Not now," Nick practically yells. "I don't want anyone to see her like this."

Once she's in bed, Sanna says, "Now? Can I call someone now?"

"Let me get her a bit cleaned up first," says Nick.

There is something so childlike, and, at the same time old, ancient, risen from a buried place, in Nick's face as he says this.

"Do you want me to help you?"

"No. I can do it by myself," he says.

She hesitates and then goes to her room. Takes out the iPad. Plugs in the adapter and flash drive.

"Mom," she whispers. "Help me figure out what to do."

ᎣᏅᏬᎠ

God
unelanvhi
and
fun
uwotlvdi
become
nature
unelanvuwotlv
and
God
unelanvhi
and
guard
agatiya
(also connected to
wait
agatisdia)
become
providence
unelanvhiagatiya.

8.

Sanna stares at the panel for a long time. At first, she tries to link the patterns to the circles in the earlier panels and can't figure it out.

And then she remembers the word she learned in geometry class: fractals.

The patterns within patterns that nature makes. Her mom was obsessed with them. Actually cried once, soon after the presidential election, while watching a documentary about them. Was her mom working on the panels even then?

Things are quiet down the hall. She supposes Nick is all right taking care of his mom. It's almost a fractal, she thinks, his being with his mom and her being with hers through the art.

But it doesn't make sense. What is her mom trying to say? She decides to flip to the next panel, and then it ends.

She clicks on the file again, searching for more. Nothing.

She scrolls through them again.

Circle.

Warrior.

Justice.

Fight.

Hurt.

Body.

God.

That's it? she thinks. Seven panels? That's not a book. That's not enough.

And then she remembers. Seven is a sacred number for the Cherokee. There are seven clans. She recognizes the totems for each of the clans in the panels. There are also seven directions: east, south, west, north, above, below, and center. Maybe seven means something else, too?

Sanna goes to the browser and types in "seven sacred number for Cherokee." She is scrolling through a page when she comes upon this phrase: "The words only have an effect when they are said aloud."

She clicks back to the last panel. She considers reading the whole panel, but she remembers what Nick told her about the Ring Fight, and she wants no English right now. She feels stupid and is not sure she is doing this right, but she wants her mother's help.

So she places her finger on each Cherokee word in the last panel and says it out loud.

"Unelanvhi."

"Uwotlvdi."

"Unelanvuwotlv."
"Unelanvhi."
"Agatiya."
"Agatisdia."
"Unelanvhiagatiya."
And then she hears Nick scream.

9.

Sanna rushes down the hallway toward the bedroom as Nick calls her name. Toward their moms' room. Parker's room now.

"What is it?" she says, breathless, to Nick.

"It wasn't wine. On my mom's shirt. I thought it was wine. It's blood."

"Blood?"

"I washed her face and was rubbing her back and then decided to change her out of the dirty clothes, and as I took off her shirt, I saw her wrist was cut."

Sanna looks down and the blood is dark on her arm like the few red leaves left on the dogwood tree.

"We've got to call an ambulance," she says.

"They'll take her away from us. And they'll separate us," says Nick. "I'm not eighteen. Sanna, we've got to stay together. Do you know what they'll do? They'll send me back to my dad."

Sanna hasn't thought of that. He's right. And where would she go? Foster care? She's heard horror stories. But Parker. They have to help Parker.

"We've got to call someone," Sanna says. Her voice cracks. She wishes her mom were there. But if her mom were there, none of this would be happening. In that moment, looking at Parker's arm covered with red blood, Sanna truly feels her mother's death.

"Eden," Nick says. "Let's call Eden."

"Eden?" That makes no sense to Sanna. Cecie, yes. She's a therapist. Hadassah, yes. She's shown she will protect them. But Eden?

"She knows plants and stuff, right?" says Nick. "She might be able to help my mom. Heal her. I don't know how much blood she's lost."

His face has the look of the hopeful boy in it again.

"Your mom never gave me her number. I just met her at the arboretum, remember?"

"Shit," he says.

"Wait," Sanna says. "Where's your mom's phone?" She goes back to the kitchen and there it is, by the empty wine bottles, and she picks it up and hurries back to the bedroom with it.

She has it unlocked and is scrolling through the contacts when Nick says, "How do you know her code?"

"It's your birthday. It wasn't too hard to figure out. I cracked it when I wanted Hadassah's number."

"Man, Squirta, you're an outlaw."

It makes her grin even though she's starting to panic a little bit. "Damn it, I can't remember Eden's last name."

"Just type her first name into the contacts and it'll come up."

"Oh, yeah."

There it is.

"Can you talk?" she says, handing the phone to him. "I don't know what to say."

"Some outlaw," he says, taking the phone from her.

She watches as he waits for someone to answer.

"Oh, Asher. I thought I was dialing Eden's number."

"I see. Well, is she there? Can I talk to her?"

He mouths the words "land line" to Sanna as he waits for Asher to get Eden. They shake their heads.

"Eden," he says. "This is Nick Jones. Parker's son. I was wondering … well, I don't know how else to say this. It seems like my mom has attempted suicide and I was wondering if you could come help."

He hangs up. "She'll be right over. She knows where we live. She said your mom held a meeting of The ReSisters here once when Mom took us to the Civil Rights Museum in Atlanta."

"I thought my mom had to work that weekend," Sanna says. That's why she couldn't go."

"I thought so, too."

10.

Eden and Asher don't knock, just come in since the door is still unlocked from when Nick and Sanna rushed in at the sound of Parker's wailing. Asher goes directly to the kitchen to put the kettle on to boil water. Eden heads back to the bedroom and asks Nick to move down and wait at the foot of the bed.

First, she opens up her bag and takes out a white embroidered cloth, places it on the bed.

In the place where her mother used to sleep, Sanna thinks. Her mother used to be the medicine.

Then Eden takes out three small brown colored bottles and little muslin bags, a fresh bundle of sage, a lighter, and a copper bowl.

She lights the sage and waves it around the room. East, south, west, and north, then up, and down, and in the center. The seven sacred directions. Sanna breathes in the scent and feels her mother's presence with them.

Eden places the sage in the copper bowl and then adds a clove of garlic to it, crushes it, and waves the smelly, smoky mixture under Parker's nose.

Immediately, Parker's eyes pop open.

"There you are," Eden coos to her gently. "Your baby Nick called me. I'm here to help."

Parker looks around the room, sees Nick and Sanna and then Asher coming in with the hot kettle and a mug.

Eden sprinkles cinnamon and ginger and cardamom into the mug and pours hot water over it, places it on the bedside table next to Parker. "We'll let that steep a little while, okay? Now let me take a look at your arm."

Parker holds her arm out. She is only wearing a cami and most of the blood is dried but some drops are still fresh in places.

Eden sprinkles cayenne pepper over the arm, gently rubs it into the wound.

Parker's eyes go wide.

"Stings a bit, eh?" Eden says. "That's okay. The hurt lets you know it's working. That's how hurt heals."

Eden looks at Nick. "Do you all have a fire pit in the yard?" she asks.

"Yeah. Why?"

"I'm going to give her a bath after she drinks this tea. I want you to take the clothes she was wearing today and burn them. Can you do that? Asher will help you make the fire if you want. Sanna will stay with me."

"Okay, I guess," Nick says.

"You guys go get started. Sanna will bring you the clothes in a bit," she says.

They leave. Sanna is impressed by how Eden has taken charge. She'd like to be in charge like that someday.

Parker has still not said anything, but she sits up a little, obviously responding to the care she's receiving from Eden. Eden hands her the mug and tells her to drink.

"Hot," Parker whispers. Her voice is deep and rough from all the crying.

"Good," says Eden. And then, "Sanna, honey, can you go boil more water in the kettle? Maybe in a big pot, too? We'll draw her a bath, but I want it to be as hot as possible."

By the time Sanna returns with the boiling water, Parker's eyes are bright and she's out of her clothes, covered with only a sheet, the comforter and blankets thrown to the side, and sweating.

"The tea is working," says Eden. "We want to stimulate her circulation. The sweating will help the blood to get moving again after the shock. The bath will help, too."

Sanna just nods and Eden hands her Parker's clothes. "Take these to the guys," she says.

Sanna is grateful to see that the fire is already lit as she steps from inside the house, warm from the boiling water and steaming bath, into the back yard, where the first real chill of November is underway.

"How's it going in there?" Nick asks her as Asher takes the clothes from her.

"Good," she says, watching the flames giving off their wrinkly patterns of heated air in the orange glow of sunset. "She seems better."

"Eden is a gifted healer," Asher says. "I don't know how I would have made it through my transition without her."

"Transition," Sanna says out loud. "That is a good word for what we are all going through."

"Yeah," says Asher. "It's true. Life is full of transition. It's just that some are accepted—normalized—by society and others aren't."

"I remember the difference it made when our moms could get married legally," Nick says. "I hadn't realized before what the social acceptance would mean."

Asher nods. "It's still not very accepted for a woman to become a man."

"But the social definitions vary, too. Right, Sanna?" Nick tries to draw her in. "Your mom taught us that the moon is male and the sun is female in Cherokee, right? Think of the implications of that."

She nods but she's not in the mood for cultural critique.

"Well, we have to live in the world we're given," Asher continues. "And Eden was amazing. It was hard for her, I know it was. But she never blamed me. I don't know if that makes sense. But I've come to feel that blame is the ultimate death sentence for a relationship. And ours is stronger than ever, despite the changes, because she never treated me as if I were at fault."

Sanna finds his use of the word "death" upsetting at a time like this and says, "I better get back in to help."

"Come give us updates when you can," says Asher.

"Okay."

Back in the house, Parker is in the bath, and the water is a weird white color.

"What's in it?" Sanna asks Eden.

"Ghee," she says. "Milk fat."

"Isn't that something that's used in Indian food?" Sanna asks.

"That's right. It's clarified butter. Absorbed by the skin, it'll aid with healing and restoration of the circulatory system."

Sanna is glad to see that Parker's arm isn't bleeding any more, but it's kind of weird seeing her naked like this, so she asks if there's anything else she can be doing.

"Sure, thanks. Can you change the sheets on the bed?" Eden says.

As Sanna does this, she thinks of the day they went to visit her mom, how she made her bed, but hadn't since. Maybe an unmade bed is a kind of fractal, she thinks. Maybe keeping it unmade sent a signal to the universe that she still needed her mom. Maybe making the bed that day somehow brought about her mother's death. It's crazy thinking, she knows, and shakes her head to try to clear it from these thoughts.

When the water in the bath begins to cool a bit, Eden brings Parker back to the freshly made bed, helps her get into clean white pajamas, and tucks her in. Then she gently pushes one sleeve up and begins to rub some oil on the wound.

"What's that?" Sanna asks.

"A mixture of aloe, myrrh, comfrey, and yellow dock."

Sanna only knows a couple of these. Her mom has given her aloe for a sunburn. "Myrrh?" she asks. "Like the three wise men brought to baby Jesus?"

"The very same. Myrrh appears several times in the Old Testament as a sacred herb, and in the Talmud, too. It was also used in ancient Egypt as an offering to the goddess Isis because it has healing and restorative properties, especially for women. So that gift was actually for Mary."

Eden smiles as she says this.

"All stories reveal deep wisdom if you know how to read them," she says, and Sanna wonders if she knows about her mom's book.

Eden puts a bandage over Parker's arm and says to her, "You sleep now. It's going to be okay."

Sanna thinks of how Nick was repeating that over and over, and how she believes it now that Eden is saying it.

"Come on, let's go outside and let her sleep," Eden whispers to Sanna. "And we need to figure out the next steps."

11.

They are settled around the fire in the back yard, the four of them. Like the four directions, thinks Sanna, and wonders again if the words she spoke out loud are having an effect in the world.

It has gotten dark, and the sky has the tinge of sapphire that comes in November. Nick pokes at the fire with a stick, which Sanna knows has always been his favorite part of having a bonfire. He likes to see the sparks.

"Why did we burn her clothes?" he asks.

"She would always think of this day when she saw them," says Asher. "Sometimes it's best to let the past go completely so you can be whole again."

Sanna can see in the firelight that Nick is thinking this over. "We haven't even had a memorial for Tembe yet," he says. "How are we going to plan it now, with my mom like this?"

"There will be time," says Eden.

Sanna won't admit it, but she's glad. Not that Parker is falling apart, but that they are not moving forward with the memorial for her mom. She's not ready.

"We need to talk about what happens next with your mom first, Nick," Eden says. "I understand that you didn't want to call an ambulance. And I'm honored that you called me. But your mom is very sick. And you kids can't take care of her alone. And you are going to need someone to take care of you."

Eden looks at Sanna. "What about you, Sanna? How are you feeling about all of this? You haven't said much."

Sanna just wants everything to go back to the way it was. She wants it to be normal. She doesn't want this to be happening. What Asher said about letting the past go so she can be whole again is echoing in her head, and she doesn't like it. She doesn't want to let her mom go. "I don't know," she says, shaking her head.

"Yes, you do," Eden encourages her. "Part of healing is figuring out what you want to do and then finding a way to do it. Even when you don't like what you're feeling."

Sanna looks at Nick and remembers what her mom advised him to do when he was being bullied. He nods at her as if he understands what she is thinking.

"Cecie, maybe?" Sanna says. "Should we call Cecie?"

"The thing about that," Asher says, "is that as a licensed therapist, she's legally obligated to report the suicide attempt. And the fact that you kids are living here without what the state would call competent supervision."

"Crap," says Nick. "We're old enough to take care of ourselves."

"I don't want to be separated from Nick," Sanna says. She feels like he's her only family member left, but she doesn't say it out loud because she doesn't want to hurt his feelings and make him feel worse about his mom.

"There's Hadassah," Nick suggests. "She gave Sanna an iPad so she could see her mom's art."

Eden's eyebrows shoot up. "You've seen your mom's art?" she asks.

"Nick," Sanna scolds, ignoring Eden's question. "Not Hadassah. She lives alone, never married, just a cat. I don't think she suddenly wants to take care of two teenagers."

"How much power do you think you both have?" Asher asks.

They aren't sure what he is getting at. "What do you mean?" Nick says.

"I mean, if you decided not to call an ambulance because you didn't want to be separated and you didn't want to go into foster care, then do you think you can follow through with those wishes and keep yourselves together? Go to school, stay safe, keep out of trouble, act as if everything is perfectly normal?"

"That's exactly what I want," says Sanna.

"Then Eden," Asher says, turning to her. "I think we should let them do that. They're old enough to know what they want, and the state really has no right to determine what would be best for them when we know perfectly well that it wouldn't."

Eden's eyes narrow. She is listening, not rejecting the idea.

"And you, Eden," he continues, "you also know that you can help Parker more than anyone in a hospital can. They'll drug her up and make her into a zombie. Nobody wants that. I know you don't."

Eden is nodding slowly now.

"So what if we take Parker with us? She can stay at our house, you can take care of her, and Nick and Sanna can just carry on with their lives as usual? If the important thing is to get Parker the help she needs, then you can do that. I know you can, Eden. You're a healer."

He turns to Nick and Sanna and says, "So you think you're able to handle the power you're being given?"

They say yes. Out loud. At midnight. In a circle around the fire light.

12.

Nick and Sanna sleep in until the next afternoon. There is no school because it's Election Day. It's been two years since the presidential election. Even after sleeping more than twelve hours straight, they feel bleary eyed and besieged by how much has changed in their lives since that day, but determined to do all they can to restore normalcy to the situation.

They spend the afternoon cleaning up the house. Nick cleans out the fire pit while Sanna scrubs the oily bathtub. Together they clean the kitchen, washing the dishes from breakfast the day before still lying in the sink, taking out the wine bottles, and mopping the floor and countertops covered with drops of wine and blood. Once that is finished, Nick says he wants to vacuum and Sanna takes a rake and goes to gather up the remaining red leaves on the ground underneath the dogwood tree.

Around sunset, they heat up a frozen pizza and watch the beginnings of the election returns on television. It's what they would have done if their moms had been there. They don't say it out loud, but they do it to pretend that they are still with them.

After a couple hours, most of the races are still too close to call, so they retreat to their rooms and set their alarms to wake in time for school in the morning.

Sanna can't remember ever feeling so exhausted and falls asleep almost immediately.

Then wakes with a start in the pitch dark.

Covered in sweat and panting, she throws off the covers and grabs her phone to see what time it is.

4:04.

It was just a dream, she tells herself. Just a dream.

She lies back down, but the images won't stop repeating themselves in the dark of her room.

She had a gun. Like all the shooters on the news. One of those automatic weapons. Something that starts with the letter M. Like the words themselves. Mass. Murders. Over and over. She could feel the smooth metal underneath her fingers in the dream. Cold and oddly comforting. Like she could do anything she wanted. But there was only one person she wanted to do. Only one person she wanted to kill.

In her dream she saw his eyes right before she fired. Everything was there. His guilt and denial. His hate and excuses. His greed and blame. His malice and stupidity. The way, as it says in her mother's book, everything comes down to the chief.

And she pulled the trigger.

In her dream, she killed the president.

In the middle of the night, two years to the minute that his election win was announced, Sanna is still shaking from the dream as the last word in her mother's book of panels returns to her.

"Unelanvhiagatiya," she says quietly. "Providence."

She whispers it as a question, as a prayer, as a message to her mother and whomever else might be listening, including the man, who, in her mind, maybe didn't start it all, but sure is doing what he can to continue it.

All of it. Her mother's detention and then death. The detentions and deaths of all the others. The increasing violence. Police shootings. Mass shootings at schools and night clubs and concerts and churches. The whitewashing of history and numbing of the pain after each one like the lyrics to a bad country music song. The blind eye turned toward the abuse of women and children. Like Parker and Nick and that mother and son in Wyoming. The wars over territory in the west. War itself. Bombings timed for expediency and not for justice. And all the after effects of war. Ring after ring after ring.

She sees it now. The concentric circles and fractal patterns. What her mother's book means. The Ring Fight and the way it ripples through time. Her dream.

As Sanna says the word out loud again, it stands in for all of this and for what she is going to do about it. Her mother, through her brother, taught her to figure out what she is going to do about it. She doesn't want to nurture like Parker or hope like Hadassah or dialogue like Cecie or heal like Eden. All of those are western female roles. She wants to be Cherokee for once. She wants to be the sun. She wants to be a warrior.

"Unelanvhiagatiya," she says.

Providence.

Sanna is going to kill the president.

13.

They take Parker's car to school and are about to go into their first period classes when Nick says, "Shit."

"What?" she says.

"Mom's classes. Who is going to cover them?"

Sanna thinks of calling Hadassah, then decides against it.

"We've got 'til tomorrow," she says. "She doesn't teach on Wednesdays anyway. We'll think of something."

"Okay," Nick says. There are dark circles under his eyes. She wonders if he had bad dreams last night, too.

"Go be normal." She smiles at him.

"Normal," he says. And they go their separate ways from the parking lot.

Her first class is American Government. She settles into her usual seat, thinking of the irony that this should be the first class she attends today, and after taking roll, the teacher, Mr. Connor, makes an announcement.

"I know this will not interest many of you, but there are some who will find it very exciting," he says. Sanna looks down, not wanting to make eye contact with him, not wanting him to see how very tired and overwhelmed she is today.

"We've gotten a last-minute invitation to the White House."

Her head shoots up.

"Technically, the Government Club has been invited. But even if you're not a member, you can join today."

He starts to hand out the permission slips.

"Another school in the state was chosen, but their advisor is pregnant and she's been put on bed rest. So our district has been chosen."

"We're invited to the turkey pardon?" quips a boy in the first row, looking at the permission slip.

"Yes," Mr. Connor says. "The White House is inviting one high school Government Club from every state to attend the Turkey Pardon at the White House this year."

"They better not pardon that turkey president," says one boy in the back, and about half the kids laugh.

Sanna doesn't.

"The pardoning takes place on the day before Thanksgiving," Mr. Connors continues. "That's a school day, as I'm sure you know. But it would be an excused absence if you decide to go. We will take a bus up the night before and come back the same day. So you can still celebrate

Thanksgiving with your families. You just need to get these permission slips signed by tomorrow by a parent. I know it's last minute notice."

Normal, normal, normal, thinks Sanna.

Perhaps this is the answer to her prayer that she spoke. Or the spell she incanted. Or a piece of the dream she had. Was it prophecy? She doesn't know. But she takes one of the permission slips and puts it into her folder, not looking up as Mr. Connors goes to the smart board and reveals his lesson for the day.

President Kennedy's smiling face beams out to the class.

"President Kennedy was the first one to pardon a turkey," he says, and Sanna clenches her hands into fists under her desk, feeling her heart beat begin to hasten. She spends the rest of the day with a closed mouth and clenched hands.

On the way home from school in the car, Sanna can't wait any longer.

"Nick, I need to ask you something."

"What is it?" he asks.

She hesitates and then says, "Well, I know we promised to keep everything normal."

"Yeah?"

"But there's this trip. A class trip. My government teacher just announced it this morning. We can go on a bus to the White House if we want."

His eyes dart toward her for a second and then he looks back at the road as he keeps driving.

"Why would you want to do that?" he asks.

"I don't know. It seems like fun," she says.

"When would this be?" he asks.

"The day before Thanksgiving. The White House is inviting kids from one high school in each state to go."

"What for?"

"To see the turkey pardoning," she says.

He laughs out loud. It's the first time she's heard him really laugh in a long time. "Squirta, that's the dumbest thing I've ever heard," he says.

"I know," she says. "I know it sounds stupid, but I really want to do it. I feel like I need to see him. Not just on television. I want to see him in person. The man who caused my mother to die."

"He didn't technically," Nick says.

"You know what I mean."

He thinks it over. They're almost at the house now.

"Look, I really need to do this," she says. "All I need from you is to sign Parker's name on the permission slip."

"Outlaw," he says.

"Yeah. So will you do it?"

They are driving down their street now and see two cars out front.

"What the—" he says.

"Nick," she pleads. "Will you do it?"

Two of the cars have government-issued license plates. State of North Carolina and Washington, D.C.

"What in the absolute fuck," Nick says, pulling into the driveway.

Sanna looks up at the front porch. Cecie is there. Another woman she doesn't know, holding a clipboard. And a man. Wearing a dark suit. Every hair in place. Grinning.

"Fuck fuck fuck," says Nick, banging the steering wheel.

"Nick, what is it?"

"That's my fucking dad," he says.

14.

"Dad, what are you doing here?" Nick asks, slamming the car door behind him.

"How are you doing," says Cecie, touching Sanna lightly on the shoulder as they wait on the porch for Nick to unlock the front door to the house.

Sanna doesn't answer, glances quickly at the woman with the clipboard. Wary.

"You sure have gotten tall," says the senator to Nick. Sanna can't bring herself to think of him as Nick's dad. He's just someone she's seen on television. An apologist for the administration. And not someone she wants in her house.

They stand around in the living room until Nick says again, "I asked you. What are you doing here?"

"Let's sit down," says Cecie.

Sanna scurries to be next to Nick on the couch, and Cecie sits on the other side of her. Senator Jeff Jones spreads his legs as he takes the wingback chair, and the clipboard woman sits on the loveseat across from them.

"I'm here, son, because your mom called me," Senator Jones declares.

"No, she didn't."

"Oh, yes, she certainly did. Yesterday afternoon. In quite a funk, too. Slurring her words and not making sense."

Nick and Sanna look at each other.

"Where is Parker now?" the senator asks. It feels like an investigation. Sanna supposes it is.

Nick says nothing.

"Come on, now, boy. I asked you a question. I came all this way because your mother called me, and she was in quite a state, and I am your father and I need an answer."

"Cecie," Nick says quietly. "I have not seen this man in almost ten years. He does not have custody of me. Do I have to speak to him?"

"Nick, I think we all want what's best for everyone," Cecie starts to say, and the senator interrupts her.

"I am your goddamned father, no matter what your crazy mother has said about me, and I am here to get some answers."

Sanna can feel Nick's body cowering uncontrollably on the couch next to her. It makes her angry. Everything about this whole situation makes her seethe with untenable anger, and she speaks up.

"Senator Jones," she says, looking directly at him. "Parker is going through a very bad time right now. Maybe she called you yesterday. But she wasn't thinking clearly. My mother has recently been killed. In a detention center. Run by your administration. I don't think she'd want to see you. And it looks as if Nick doesn't want to see you, either."

"I understand what you're saying," says Cecie to Sanna. "But we have to get some answers. If Parker is not here, where is she?"

"She's staying with Eden," Nick says.

"Who the hell is Eden? Another one of the lesbians?" the senator guffaws.

"Please, Senator Jones," Cecie urges. "We have to be respectful."

Senator Jones crosses his arms across his chest and glares at her.

"Nick, why is your mom with Eden?" Cecie asks gently.

"Eden is helping her." That's all he says.

"I see." Cecie takes a deep breath and sighs. "Okay. Well, let me explain why I'm here. I am here because your dad called Child Protective Services after your mom called him and filed a report."

She nods to the woman in the loveseat who looks up from taking notes as Cecie continues. "This is Dondra Baker. She's with CPS, and she was kind enough to call me."

"How did she know to call you?" Sanna asks Cecie.

"That's not important right now," Cecie says. "What's important is that she has some questions to ask you, and," Cecie says the next words very slowly, "it's important that you answer them honestly."

"Thank you, Cecie," Dondra Baker says. "As Cecie said, I'm here to make sure that you children are safe. I understand that you've lost a mother, and I'm very sorry for your loss."

Senator Jones shifts in his seat.

"And I understand that your other mom has been having a hard time dealing with the grief."

No one says anything.

"The thing is, if she is not able to take care of you, we will have to find suitable adults. And usually, the birth parent is the first one we call. In this case, the fact that Mr. Jones reached out to our office shows that he is concerned for your welfare."

"He's not my birth parent," says Sanna. "I'm not going anywhere with him."

"Me, either," says Nick. "I won't leave Sanna, either."

"You'll do what I damn well say," the senator spits.

"Sir." Ms. Baker holds up a hand toward him. "Please."

She turns back toward them. "I'd like to interview you separately if you don't mind. Cecie can be in the room with you if you like. That's why

I called her. We like to have a therapist who knows the family to serve as a witness."

Sanna pictures this. "I don't need Cecie in my interview," she says. She doesn't want Nick to be left alone with his dad.

Cecie pats her hand. "I understand. Do you want to go first then?"

"Okay. Sure. Where?"

"Is there a kitchen table, maybe?"

Sanna thinks about a poem that Parker showed her once at breakfast. Something about how the world will end at a kitchen table.

She stands up, sincerely hoping her world is not about to end.

The bits of her world that aren't already dead.

15.

"You can call me, Dondra, okay?"

"Okay."

"I'm going to start with some basic questions."

"Okay."

"Full name?"

"Sanna Marie Penbrook."

"Age?"

"15."

"Date of birth?"

"December 2, 2002."

"Mother's name?"

"Tembe Penbrook."

"No middle name?"

"She doesn't use it."

"I need it anyway."

"Warmaker."

"Warmaker?" Dondra looks up.

"That's why she doesn't use it." Sanna smiles. No use letting the woman think she's unkind.

"Okay. Do you know her date of birth?"

"November 21, 1967."

"Date of death?"

Sanna thinks back. Sunday was the 4th.

"The fourth."

"Just this past Sunday?" Dondra asks. Sanna nods. She's not sure if this is good or bad in the eyes of the social worker.

"Father's name?"

"I don't know."

"You don't know?"

"My parents weren't married. I never met him. He's not on my birth certificate." I'm a bastard, she thinks, but doesn't say it out loud. A bastard and an orphan.

"Okay. Any other relatives live nearby?"

"No," says Sanna. "My grandma passed away a few years ago."

"And Parker has adopted you?"

"Yes. She's my mom."

"How do you feel about your mom?"

"I love her."

"I mean, how do you feel about her now? How do you feel about how she has been handling everything?"

Sanna thinks back to the night before, the way Eden cared for her. The way she needed it.

"I think she needs Eden right now," Sanna says carefully. "I think it's best for her to stay with Eden." She realizes she hasn't really answered the question.

"And you know you can't stay with your brother alone in the house, right? So do you have a preference about where to go?"

"I don't want to go anywhere. It's my house."

"I know. But my job is to determine where you can stay that will be safe."

"This is safe. Safer than sending us with him," Sanna says. "Nick told me that he has been abusive with him. And with Parker. I can't believe she called him." She is so angry at Parker for doing that, but she stops herself before saying it out loud.

She knows the power of saying things out loud.

"Okay," Dondra says. "I can't really write down hearsay in the report. So I'll need to talk to Nick about that. Is there anything you'd like to ask me?"

Sanna suddenly has an idea. "Hadassah," she says.

"What?"

"Hadassah Seigel. She's my mother's best friend. Maybe we can stay with her."

"Okay," Dondra says. "Now we're getting somewhere. Do you have her number?"

Sanna smiles and takes out her phone. "I sure do."

16.

While Dondra interviews Nick with Cecie in the kitchen, Sanna makes a beeline for her bedroom and locks the door. She doesn't even like having that man in the house and there's no way she's going to be alone in a room with him.

She flops on her bed, turns on a light, and takes the iPad out of her backpack.

"Mom," she whispers. "Help me."

And then she has an idea. Goes to her bookshelf and gets a big notebook her mom gave her last Christmas, and some pens. She was into graphic novels back then and her mom encouraged her to make her own. She never did.

She opens the notebook and draws seven circles, one for each panel in her mom's book. And then she thinks back to the first seven people she talked to after finding out that her mom had been detained.

The first one was Parker. So that's Circle #1. She writes Parker's name next to that circle. She glances back at her mother's panel.

"You can't make it," she reads.

Parker is her mother, but Sanna can't count on her right now, and she knows she is not alone in this. Nick is with her, too. And many other children who have had to accept this.

She draws an X through the first circle.

The second person she talked to was Nick. Sanna flips to the next panel.

"Warrior," Sanna whispers, and draws two concentric circles inside Circle #2 and writes Nick's name beside it. She thinks of Nick's story about the Ring Fight.

She could just stop here, she thinks, and assume that this is the sign she is looking for, but her mom would want her to keep going. Figure out all the perspectives that are possible before deciding definitively.

The third person she went to was Hadassah. She writes down her name and then looks at the third panel. Of course. Justice. That is what Hadassah represents. And the star. Six points. Like the Star of David. And also for the Cherokee Nation.

She draws the star inside the circle and moves to the next one.

Cecie was the next person she talked to. Sanna writes her name and then clicks to the next panel.

Hurt.

The broken circle. And Cecie's belief in the healing power of speech. As Sanna draws a line through the fourth circle, she pictures the wound on Parker's arm and the tears that fell from her eyes and how it wasn't speech she needed or could even handle that night. It was something else.

Eden. That was the fifth person that Sanna went to for advice. The fifth panel is about fighting, but not in the way we think of fighting. Using your feet. Moving. Acting. Showing up. She thinks about how Eden showed up that night for them, for Parker and for them.

She's not sure what to put in this circle, but then it hits her: the feet. The feet that do the running away and the feet that do the showing up. They are the same feet. She sketches feet inside the circle and writes Eden's name next to it.

The sixth person, Sanna realizes, has to be Asher. That night at dinner at their house, and then that night around the fire. He added the element that allowed everything to click into place for Sanna. She turns to the next panel.

The word "funds" jumps out at her. Money. Power. How these are connected to both nation and anarchy. She realizes she has to have all of this if she is going to carry out her plan.

She writes Asher's name and draws coins in the sixth circle.

And then she clicks to the seventh panel. This panel, about God and providence, and the guarding and waiting that connect them, Sanna decides, is about her mom.

She rubs the tip of her pen across the end of her right index finger and then stamps her fingerprint in the middle of the circle.

Making a seal. A promise. She knows she can do it. She just doesn't know yet how it is going to get done.

She jumps as Nick startles her by knocking on the door.

"Squirta?" he says. "Can I come in?"

17.

Sanna gets up to unlock the door and let him in.

As she locks the door again, he moves toward the bed and picks up the notebook.

"What's this?" he asks quietly.

"A plan," she admits.

She's about to tell him everything, and then she changes her mind. "What happened in your interview?" she asks.

He sits down at her desk.

"I have to go with him."

"What?" she exclaims.

"They're making me."

"They can't do that!"

"They can."

"Oh, this makes me so angry," Sanna says, glancing at her notebook. "I thought we were going to stay together."

"I wanted to. But we can't. And it makes me angry, too."

"How angry?"

"Very. I'm sick of being scared of him. I can't be that scared little boy any more."

"It's like we're not allowed to be kids anymore," Sanna says.

"I know," he says. "But I feel like it's time for me to stand up."

"Maybe it is for me, too," says Sanna, whispering.

She holds up her hand, bending her pointer finger with the dark ink at the tip and thinking about how he can't do this because of his father, and motions for him to sit next to him on the bed. She thinks about Speakfinger as she does it.

He moves closer.

She shows him the seven circles with her sketches, picks up her pen, and writes at the bottom.

I want to kill the president.

His eyes go wide. He tilts his head.

"The field trip to D.C.?" he whispers. "Is that why you wanted to go?"

She nods. She doesn't know if she's doing the right thing by telling him. He could try to stop her. He could tell someone. The whole family could be locked up in a nut house before too long. He might be the only one left. She waits. Doesn't rush him. She can tell he is thinking long and hard.

"If I go with my dad," he says slowly. "I might be able to have better access."

He takes the notebook from her, looks at the circles. Looks at his name and puts his finger in the middle of the circle next to it.

"But it might be harder for me to get what we need," he whispers.

"We?"

"I want to help you," he says. "It'll be the way we stay together."

Sanna is glad he wants to help her but she's not sure she is being fair to him in allowing him to get involved. It's her plan. It's her responsibility.

But it's too late. She can see on his face that he has made up his mind. He reaches over for the pen still in her hand, takes it, and writes below what she has written.

I want to kill the senator.

18.

They hear the doorbell ring, and Sanna takes the notebook back from Nick, rips out the page, and tears it up, stuffs it into her dirty clothes hamper and picks it up.

"What are you doing?" he says.

"Laundry," she says and unlocks the door.

She ignores the people gathering at the front door and goes back to the laundry room, throws her clothes in the washer and turns it on.

"Mom!" she hears Nick say from the living room and goes to join them.

"Parker," Sanna says, and hugs her.

"What are you doing here?" Nick asks her.

"Your dad called me," she says. "He told me he was here and that Child Protective Services was about to give you to him. I couldn't let that happen."

Sanna notices she is wearing a loosely fitting long-sleeved shirt. Sanna doesn't recognize it. Eden probably gave it to her. To cover the cuts.

"How did you get here?" Nick asks, looking out the window.

"Uber."

Sanna isn't sure she's telling the truth. She thinks it's more likely that Eden brought her, but she doesn't say anything.

"How are you doing, Parker?" Cecie asks.

"I'm fine," Parker says. "I am. There's no reason for everyone to be alarmed. I just …"

She looks to Nick and Sanna and continues. "I just had too much to drink. I've been so upset about everything. My friend Eden came to help me. I stayed at her house. It's not the end of the world. It was just a couple nights."

"You're in no shape to take care of these kids. They should both come with me. I have a nice wife," he says, a sharp edge in his voice. "They can have two parents. Two stable parents who can take care of them."

"I'm not sure …," Cecie begins to say.

"Bullshit," Parker says, her gaze boring into him. "Over my dead body. And one dead body in this family, thanks to your government, is quite enough, thank you very much."

"I had nothing to do with that," he says.

"The hell you didn't. Don't you dare think I don't know whose side you're on. And it certainly isn't the side of me and my family."

"I'm on the side of the nation," he says, almost as if he can't stop himself. Sanna has seen him use this tone of voice on television.

"Get the hell out of my house," Parker says.

No one moves.

Parker turns to the social worker, glances at her badge. "He has had a restraining order issued against him. Ten years ago. Did you know that, Ms. Baker? Did you even check to see about that?" She's almost spitting. "Or do you just assume that a great senator is innocent?"

"Ma'am," Dondra says, "I really don't think —"

"You all don't think," Parker says, and the doorbell rings again. "Oh, great, what fresh hell is this?"

Sanna thinks that Parker better calm down, and soon, if she's going to convince CPS that she's fit to take care of them.

"It's probably Dr. Seigel," Dondra says. "I telephoned her after I interviewed Sanna. She said she'd like to stay with her."

Parker swirls toward Sanna. "What?"

"You weren't here," Sanna says.

Cecie answers the door and Hadassah comes in.

"Parker," she says. "You're here."

"Of course I'm here. This is my home."

Hadassah walks over to Sanna. "How are you?"

"Fine," Sanna says. What else can she say?

"Look," the senator says, "I'm not sticking around while all the members of your coven show up. I have work to do. It's time to make a decision."

Dondra looks at all of them. Then she says to Parker, "We don't remove the minors from the home when there is a parent present unless there is a clear and present danger. We wait for a second home visit. So I see no reason to do anything but let Nick and Sanna be with their mom, and it's time for me to leave."

Dondra reaches down to get her bag.

"You don't have to ask me twice," the senator says. "I'm going, too. But I swear, the next time, I'm pressing charges. My son shouldn't have to live with a mad woman."

He lets Dondra leave first — such a gentleman — and then slams the door as he leaves. Cecie and Hadassah start toward the door.

"Wait," Parker says quietly. "I need to talk to the two of you."

The women hesitate and then sit. Parker takes the wingback chair where the senator had been.

"I want to apologize. To all of you. You especially, Nick and Sanna. I am sorry for not handling Tembe's death more gracefully. I really messed up. And I'm sorry."

Nick goes to her and hugs her. "It's okay, Mom."

"It's not okay. And I'm going to make it up to you. I've been thinking about the memorial service. The chapel on campus is booked all week, but I've asked Eden and she says we can use the arboretum Friday afternoon. We don't have the ashes yet. They're saying they need more time for the forensic evaluation. But I think we need to go ahead with this. I think we need this. Will you come?"

Everyone nods.

"Hadassah," Parker says. "Will you lead the service? Something simple. That's all she would have wanted."

"Of course."

"Good. Thank you. Nick? Sanna? Will you say something? Share a memory, maybe?"

They nod.

"Okay," Parker smiles. "Well, I'm back. Who's hungry? I have some frozen pizzas and some salad. Stay for dinner? Please? I'll call Eden and Asher. We'll have a wake."

"A wake?" Sanna asks.

"It's an Irish thing. You gather together before a funeral. And eat. And drink. A lot." She pauses, laughs a little. "But not tonight. Tonight we'll just eat. Okay?"

And everyone agrees.

19.

The next day at breakfast, Sanna feels like she is sleep-eating. The group stayed late the night before, and they were loud. There was drinking even though Parker said there wouldn't be, so even though Sanna excused herself and went to her room soon after dinner, she didn't get much sleep.

And the sleep she had was filled with dreams. Dreams of a creature, half-man, half-six-point buck in their back yard, chewing on Hadassah's cat, Winston. Blood all over his mouth. Sanna remembers it now and gets up to pour her cereal down the sink, stomach queasy.

Parker says it would be okay for them to stay home from school, but Nick and Sanna say together that they want to go. They've missed too much school already. Sanna actually doesn't want to miss the chance to turn in the permission slip for the trip to D.C. And she can't wait to talk to Nick alone.

"Such good kids," Parker smiles and sips her coffee. "Oh, I was wondering if you could take Tembe's truck to school today. I have some errands I need to run before the memorial service tomorrow and you know it doesn't get good gas mileage."

"Sure, mom," Nick says, and they go to their rooms to get dressed.

"Sanna, wait," she says. "I did a load of laundry this morning, and your clothes were in the washer, all wet, with pieces of paper all through it."

"Oh my gosh," Sanna says. "I'm sorry. I forgot to put them in the dryer when everyone came over. And ...."

Nick watches her from the doorway. "I guess I left some paper in a pocket. I'm sorry."

"It's okay," Parker says. "It was kind of meditative to pick through the pieces this morning before putting the clothes in the dryer."

Tembe would have made her do it herself. Parker is too nice. Sanna sees this clearly now, and Sanna is done with nice.

"I should have done it myself, Parker. I'm so sorry."

On the way to school Nick rags her for the mistake.

"What if the writing had still been visible, Sanna?"

"Don't raise your voice at me," she says. She sees traces of his father in him now, after having met him. And it scares her. But she refuses to give in to the fear. "I made a mistake. It won't happen again."

"It better not," he says. "We have to be careful. If we're going to go through with this."

"I know."

"You still want to go through with it?"

"Of course. That's why I'm going to school today. To turn in that permission slip. You'll sign your mom's name on it, won't you?"

"Sure," he says. "But I'm dropping you off. I'm not going to school."

"Why?"

"I'm meeting someone."

"Who?" Sanna wishes for a second that she hadn't told him. She wishes she were doing this all on her own. She feels Nick taking over. The whole point of this is to fight back against people who take over.

"I won't tell you. You don't need to know. But it's someone who can help me with what we're going to do."

Nick signs his mom's name on the paper while they are pulled over on the side of the road a block before school.

"I don't want anyone to see me at school," he says. "Especially in this truck."

He is not talking about being embarrassed by her mom's truck, as clunky and old as it is, but by being seen before driving away to do whatever he is going to do.

"That's fine. I'll walk," she says. "Please be careful?"

"Don't worry," he says.

But Sanna will worry. It feels as if she's become a worry stone, alternating between feelings of numbness and anxiety.

And once again, she thinks of Spearfinger with her skin of stone like the boulders in the mountains around Cherokee. Did Spearfinger have a loss so great that she, too, turned to stone?

20.

When Sanna arrives at the arboretum on Friday afternoon, it looks different than the last time she was there. Someone has made garlands of chrysanthemums in white and orange and hung them, branch to branch, along the walkway among the trees.

It's just a small thing, but it changes the way Sanna sees the place. Highlights the interaction between humans and nature here.

She spots Eden. "Did you do all this?" she asks, pointing to the garlands.

"I did. Parker told me these were your mom's favorite colors."

"Yes," Sanna says, "they were." She forces herself to say the word in the past tense.

"You look beautiful," Eden says, smiling.

"Thank you," says Sanna, looking down at her mauve velvet dress. Her mother gave it to her for her birthday last year, and it's a bit snug, but actually looks quite good on her. "Where's Parker?" Sanna asks.

"I last saw her at the altar," Eden says.

"Altar?"

"Asher built it when your mom decided to have the service here. It's over near where we sat that day."

"Oh. Okay." Sanna starts to walk away and then turns back. "Eden?"

"Yes?"

"Thank you for everything."

Eden smiles. It's a sweet smile, and there are tears in her eyes. "You're welcome, honey."

Eden heads back to the office and points her in the direction of the altar.

The altar is not what Sanna expects.

It's a circle of stones. Boulders, more like it. The circle encloses a much larger stone in the center.

Sanna thinks of her mom's book. Circles in circles.

"How do you like it?" Parker asks her.

"It's great," Sanna says, even though it looks a little goth to her. A little like a place where a sacrifice would take place.

"Asher's a great guy," says Parker, and Sanna nods.

"So how is this going to go?" Sanna asks.

"I'm not sure," Parker admits. "Hadassah said she'd handle it. If you want to say something, you'll have a chance."

"I wrote something at school," Sanna says.

"Oh, Sanna," Parker says. "You really didn't have to go to school today, you know."

"I know. I wanted to. I want to keep things normal."

"You're like your mom that way," Parker says. "She never was very good with emotion. I mean, she was emotional, but she preferred to show it through action. Find some project to throw herself into. You know what I mean?"

Sanna nods. This is exactly what she's doing. And she takes it as a sign that she is doing the right thing.

People are starting to gather, and Parker tells them they will be standing in a circle around the altar. There are professors from the college and students, some people from town, but not too many. It was a last-minute thing, and Sanna knows Parker didn't want a large crowd anyway.

Hadassah arrives, wearing a beautiful camel-colored wool suit. She has a few papers in her hands, and an orange mum pinned to her lapel. That's a nice touch, Sanna thinks, and then she notices that Eden has a basket of mum corsages that she's handing out to everyone. Sanna takes a white one. She can smell the tangy smell on her fingers after she pins it to her dress. It reminds her of her mother, outside gardening almost every weekend. Planting mums because they keep the mosquitos away.

"Thank you for joining us here today," Hadassah says, looking at the people circled around.

"Where's Nick?" Parker whispers to Sanna.

Sanna looks around. She knows that he skipped school again today, but she can't believe that Nick would miss this. Where can he be?

Hadassah begins to talk about death.

"Each religion has stories about death," she says. "These stories can be scary. They can be miraculous. They can bring comfort. They can promise a second chance. I looked through stories from many cultures in trying to prepare something to say today. But then I realized that Tembe was about something much deeper than words."

She pauses and looks to the stone next to her.

"Tembe would have loved this," she says. "Thank you, Asher."

He nods.

"To Tembe, the whole world was a work of art. When I first met her, one of the first things she told me was that she saw patterns in everything."

Sanna thinks of the fractals in the panel about God.

"That is what an artist does," Hadassah continues. "Sees the patterns. Recreates these patterns for others to see. Allows us to see, in the beauty of the patterns, how our lives are connected to everything that came before and will come after, and know that this is what brings our lives meaning."

Hadassah puts her hand over her orange mum and asks everyone to do the same.

"Tembe is symbolized by these mums," she says. "It was her favorite flower, and it is associated with autumn. Tembe's birthday was in the autumn, and so was her death. So the symbolism of the falling leaves, the muted colors, the drying ground, these are also Tembe. Autumn reminds us of impermanence. Art works as a counterbalance to this."

Hadassah taps the flower near her heart, and then unpins it.

"Each of us has a flower. It is a different flower. And each of us has a different relationship to Tembe. Separately we are alone in our grief. When we cling to our flower, we have only something impermanent. This flower will wilt and dry. Its color will fade."

Hadassah places her flower on the ground.

"But when we bring our flowers together," she says, pointing to the circle, "we create art. We honor Tembe. We bring beauty and meaning to the world through the pattern we make."

Parker steps forward from the circle of people and lays her flower on the ground by Hadassah's. Sanna moves to do the same, and chooses a spot a bit above both Parker's and Hadassah's, women who have been like mothers to her, creating a triangle with them underneath her to support her.

As everyone moves slowly around the altar, creating a pattern with all the individual flowers, Parker whispers to Sanna, "Text Nick. I can't believe he's not here."

Sanna is worried, too. But she doesn't have her phone with her. Before the final chrysanthemum is placed on the ground, Sanna goes to Asher.

"Can you text Nick for me?" she whispers. "Ask him where he is?"

"What's the number?" he asks, and she tells him.

Sanna goes back to stand next to Parker.

Parker cocks her head toward Asher for an answer. He shakes his head.

"Now, if Parker would like to say something," Hadassah says, stepping out of the circle and letting Parker take her place.

"Tembe was," Parker begins, "the love of my life." Her voice cracks; she looks down at the swirls and patterns of flowers at her feet, and regains her steadiness. "She was an artist. You all know that. But what I want to say is that she was an artist who worked in the medium of love, too. She was there for me in a way no one ever has been."

She pauses and her eyes fill up with tears. "And she was strong. Stronger than I will ever be. Many of you know that Tembe was a single mother for the first five years of Sanna's life. But she talked about those years not as a sacrifice, not as a hardship, but as the most wonderful lesson in love that she ever could have. She told me that being Sanna's mother trained her to be my wife."

Tears are falling quickly now down Parker's face. Sanna and many others are crying, too.

"She said that loving that baby, so small and vulnerable, so helpless and yet so powerful, taught her what love was."

A sob escapes and she takes a deep breath.

"I am so thankful to Sanna, my daughter, for coming into the world and helping to bring Tembe to me. I know she would be very proud of you, and I am, too. And I know that the love that Tembe showed to us will continue to make circles in the world."

Parker steps from the circle and hugs Sanna for a long time.

Sanna wipes away tears from her cheeks as she moves to take Parker's place.

Once she is next to the altar, she slips her hand into her bra where she has a little piece of paper tucked into it, and a few people laugh. Sanna laughs, too, and it helps her gain a sense of calm.

She unfolds the paper and begins to read.

"My mother was an artist," she says. "But she was also a teacher."

She looks up at Tembe's students, past and present, gathered there. And at Hadassah.

"My mother taught through her art. I don't understand all of it. But there is something I want to share with you today. It's about God."

She looks at Eden. At Hadassah again.

"I think she would have liked that we are meeting here, outside in these woods today, for her. Because the Cherokee word for nature, I recently learned, is a combination of the words for God and fun. My mother knew that, and she taught it to me."

She stops. Hesitates. Thinks about stopping there. And then continues.

"But there's another word that combines God with another word, too. When you put the words for God and guard and wait together, you get providence. And I don't want us to forget that my mom died because she was left unguarded. Our country failed to keep her safe. And I vow to God, here today, that I will not wait to guard us in the future."

She looks up from the paper. No one moves. For a moment, she regrets what she has said, but then she sees Nick behind his mom, his hands on her shoulders, and then he walks toward Sanna, hugs her, and takes her place at the center of the circle.

"Tembe was the best dad I ever had," he starts, and people laugh, glad to have a break from the heaviness of what Sanna had to say.

"Seriously. The woman was fierce. She was so strong, not just physically. I mean, she was ripped from all the yard work and yoga she did. But she was emotionally strong. For our whole family. I think she was a warrior."

He looks at Sanna.

"I want to be a warrior like Tembe," he says. "And I promise all of you that that's what I'll do."

He steps from the circle and Hadassah returns to the middle, lights sage, and begins to smudge the circle.

The scent reminds Sanna of home.

"As this smoke ascends into the air," Hadassah says. "We release our love and memories of Tembe to the world she loved so much. As its scent clings to our hair and clothes, she will cling to us, becoming part of us in her absence. This is how a seed gets carried. It falls first."

When smoke fills the circle, Hadassah returns to the center and raises her hands to the sunset colored sky.

"Join me in saying goodbye to Tembe," she says.

The people raise their hands, saying, "Goodbye. Farewell. Blessed be. Amen."

Nick has his arm around Parker who is sobbing, and Sanna feels alone until she notices Cecie next to her, opening her arms to her and saying, "Come here, child. Come here."

21.

Sanna rides with Parker back to the house where everyone has been invited for a potluck supper after Tembe's memorial.

"Do you know where Nick was? Why he was late to the memorial service?" Parker asks her.

"No," she says, but she has a guess. Not a guess she'll tell Parker, though.

"It's just not like him," Parker says, taking the turn out of the arboretum parking lot and onto the wooded winding road through campus.

"I know," Sanna says, hoping Parker will change the subject. She's nervous that Parker will notice something is different about her, too.

"And what did he mean about being a warrior? What was that about?" Parker isn't letting it go.

"I don't know," Sanna says, as convincingly as she can. "I know he respected my mom's strength. I think it was about that. He wants to be strong like she was."

Parker shakes her head. "Something is not adding up," she says. "I can always tell when he's upset about something and not letting me know."

"Well, my mom is gone," Sanna says. It's the first time she's said it out loud. It feels real when it comes from her mouth like this. And she thinks about the words she said out loud from Tembe's panels.

"Sanna," Parker says, finally switching the topic. "I want to say again how sorry I am for what happened on Monday night. I really am."

"It's okay."

"It's not okay. And you don't have to say it is." Parker turns down their street, and when Sanna sees a few cars from the memorial service already out front, she remembers coming home like this with Nick. Seeing his dad on the front porch, waiting for him.

"I'm really glad you came back," Sanna says. "That's the important thing."

Parker looks over, maybe wondering if this is a kind of forgiveness Sanna is giving her.

"I wouldn't want Nick to go with his dad. Ever," Sanna says.

Parker stops the car a few houses away from theirs. "How much do you know about Nick's dad?" she asks.

"Enough," Sanna says.

Parker looks down and says, "I will always blame myself for staying as long as I could. Your mom told me so many times that I needed to let it go. But I couldn't. I think a part of me was always afraid he would still come back for us."

"My mom would have never let that happen," Sanna says. She knows with all her heart that this is true, and feels her mother's strength to defend the family within her now, too.

"I know." Parker nods. "You're right. But when she wasn't there, and I heard about the shootings, and what he had done to that little boy …."

"It didn't happen to us," Sanna says.

"That's the thing about trauma, though," Parker says. "Other traumas bring back what happened. They make it feel like it's happening again."

"Is that why you called him?" Sanna dares to ask.

Parker looks at her, and there is something different in her eyes. A bit of the softness is gone.

"I called him because an incredible rage ignited in me. The injustice of it. That Tembe would be gone and he was still living. It just didn't seem right. A breach of justice. I wanted to tell him that. I had so many things to say to him that I had never said. I spilled it all out that night when I called him. But it put you kids in danger. What I did made him call Child Protective Services. And for Nick to have to go back to him, that's the last thing I would have wanted. I guess I wanted some kind of balance to everything. Some kind of justice."

Justice. Sanna rolls this word around in her mouth before she says it out loud. "Justice?"

Parker does not know, cannot know, what Sanna means by her question, but she answers anyway. "Justice would be for Tembe to still be alive. She never did anything to hurt anyone. And the fact that—" She shakes her head, looks actually nauseated.

"That he is still alive and she is not is gross injustice. There's no other word for it. And I don't know that anything will ever make it right."

They sit quietly for a moment. Sanna wonders if what she is planning is indeed a way to make it right, and then Parker takes her foot off the brake and they drive the remaining hundred yards to the house, pulling into the driveway where Hadassah waits with a big box of challah.

"You made all of those?" Parker exclaims, smiling.

"It's Shabbat," Hadassah says. "It seemed like the right thing to do."

As they walk through the yard where people are gathered, Sanna thinks about the morning at Hadassah's, the rugelach she made, and the challah now.

Parker cooks and bakes, too, but there's a difference when Hadassah makes it. She maintains a kind of joy in it for herself. Parker, Sanna thinks, almost does it in a way that is too much. Asks too much for people to enjoy it in order to make her happy.

For Hadassah, knowing she will enjoy it seems to be all she needs to make her happy.

Sanna remembers something from when Tembe and Parker were dating. Uncertain about upsetting the mother-daughter dyad they had created, Sanna had asked Tembe if Parker made her happy.

"No one can make you happy," Tembe had said. "That's a job for each person to do on her own."

It was a lesson that Sanna planted within herself. Maybe now it is sprouting and blooming out.

"Sanna, can you help me with the table?" Hadassah asks, pulling Sanna from her memory.

"Sure."

Hadassah pulls the seven loaves of challah from the box and then silver candle holders, a silver cup, and a bottle of wine. She places them all on the dining room table.

"What's all this?" Sanna asks.

"That is a kiddush cup," says Hadassah, pointing to the cup and then holding up the candle holder. "And this is a menorah. It comes from the time of Moses, and is on the Israeli flag. It symbolizes the six branches of knowledge that come from God."

"There are seven in all," Sanna says. "Seven is a sacred number for the Cherokee."

"There are many similarities," Hadassah says. "That's why I asked you to help me set it up. Have you had a chance to make it through your mom's book?"

"Yes. There are seven panels, and the last one is about God," Sanna says.

"Exactly. And what did you think?"

Sanna hesitates, not sure what to say. She watches Hadassah take each of the loaves out and place them around the table.

"I think it reminded me of what you said about *tikkun olam* that day," she says finally. "About taking right action to save the world."

Hadassah's eyebrows go up.

"The book made you want to save the world?" she asks. "That's quite something for a work of art to do. And how are you going to do that?"

"I'm still thinking it over." That is all Sanna says, but Hadassah looks at her curiously.

"Hadassah, do you need anything?" Parker calls from the kitchen where she is putting the last-minute touches on the chili she's been making in the slow cooker all day.

"I could use some butter and honey," Hadassah responds, and then touches Sanna lightly on the arm. "Let's talk more about this later, okay?"

Sanna is left standing by the table with the seven loaves waiting to be eaten.

"Those look beautiful," Cecie says, interrupting what she's thinking.

"Hadassah made them," Sanna says, and suddenly she is very weary. The house is filling up with people, Parker is in her element, preparing to feed them all, but Sanna just wants to be alone.

"I think I need …," she says to Cecie.

"Do you want to go with me to the back yard?" Cecie asks. "Your mom wants more wood for the fireplace."

Sanna nods, glad for an excuse to step away without seeming rude.

The cold air is refreshing as they step outside. It's time for coats now, Sanna thinks, remembering how warm it was in October when her mom left for the Netherlands, how silly it seemed that she would need to bring a coat on the plane.

"How are you doing, Sanna?" Cecie asks softly as they head back to the woodpile.

Tembe cut every piece of this wood, and Sanna wishes she could know exactly the spots where her mother's hands had been.

"I miss my mom," she says.

Cecie stops. Turns to her. "Say more?"

"I miss my mom, and I'm sad," Sanna admits. "But not as sad as I would have thought I would be. It's like this small stream that flows now and then. But most of the time, I'm really pissed off. Sorry," she says, "about swearing."

"No need. Keep going."

"I'm so angry. Really angry. And I want to do something about it."

Cecie looks back to the house. The lights are glowing inside, warm and gold, through the windows. People are laughing and talking and can be heard even from the back of the yard.

"Mourning can take different branches," Cecie says. "One branch, or stream as you called it, is sadness. I think Parker went down that branch the other night."

She pauses.

"I'm glad she came back," Cecie says. "But another stream is anger. We can want to do something, anything, to counteract the loss. Maybe that's what you're feeling?"

Sanna nods, not wanting to say too much.

"I saw Hadassah talking to you about the menorah," Cecie says, picking up a few pieces of wood and handing them to Sanna before gathering some for herself. "There are many branches in everything," she says. "It can help to remember that. This wood came from branches. Trees have branches, the blood branches in our bodies, religions have different ways of explaining what God is."

Just before they step back into the noise of the house, Cecie says, "It's just good to remember that there are many branches, and you don't want to find yourself on one of them, too far out."

Eden holds the door open for them as they bring the wood into the house, and Parker says, "There you are! I'd forgotten about the wood. Good. Hadassah is ready for Shabbat. Come on into the dining room."

They gather around the dining room table. Hadassah sings a song in Hebrew, then explains that the song welcomes the angels into the house, and that Tembe is one of the angels now. She then says she is going to sing another song, to praise the woman of the house, who is Parker, for all she has done to prepare for this night. There are tears in Parker's eyes as she says this, and Eden puts her arm around her.

Hadassah then lights the candles, singing more, and then invites everyone to take a piece of challah. The braided bread is torn into scrumptious pieces, and Hadassah explains that it's sweet but extra good with the whipped butter and honey she has made.

They eat the bread together, and then Hadassah pours some wine in the kiddush cup and says "Shabbat Shalom," and takes a sip before and passing it around for everyone to share.

As Nick takes the cup and says, "Shabbat Shalom," he looks over at Sanna across the table, and she is filled with shame.

She thinks about what Cecie said to her outside. Maybe they have gone too far on the branch of anger. Maybe they need to turn back.

Sanna knows that "shalom" is the word for peace. Is what they are planning to do really a way to bring about peace?

Justice, maybe.

What brings together the branches of peace and justice?

The blessing done, Parker begins to serve everyone bowls of chili, and Hadassah is encouraging them to have more challah and butter and honey with it. People are settling into seats in the living room, taking bites and complimenting both Parker and Hadassah on the meal.

"Parker seems so much better," says Eden quietly to Sanna as they stand in the kitchen with their bowls of chili.

"Thanks to you," Sanna says.

"Is she really, though?" Eden asks.

"I don't know. She's keeping busy, that's for sure."

Eden nods and takes a bite. "She sure can cook. Do you all have plans for Thanksgiving?"

"Actually," Sanna says. "Yes. I mean, I'm not, well, I haven't told Parker yet, but I've been invited to go to D.C. the day before Thanksgiving. To the White House for the turkey pardoning."

Eden almost blows chili across the room, laughing.

"You what!"

"Yeah. It's with my government class."

"What a riot! The irony," Eden exclaims and calls Asher over, explaining what Sanna has just told her. "Can you believe that? He's going to pardon the turkey! Man, I'd like to see that!"

"Actually," Asher says, not laughing. "We could."

"What?" Sanna and Eden both say at the same time.

"There's supposed to be a protest at the White House that day."

Sanna does not know this. How could she know this? And where is Nick? Why is he always disappearing?

"Yep," Asher continues. "Maybe we should go."

"Maybe we should," Eden says. "I wonder if anyone else would want to join us."

"Excuse me," Sanna says, suddenly feeling the need to find Nick.

He is not in the living or dining room. She looks in his room. Not there.

Where can he be?

She texts him. "Nick? Where are you?"

"I'm in your room."

Sanna looks around, hoping to make sure no one is watching her as she starts down the hallway toward her room.

What is he doing in her room? she wonders.

When she opens the door, he's standing there, grinning. It freaks her out a little bit, if she is honest with herself.

"Why are you in here?" she asks. "What's going on? And why haven't you gone to school the last two days?"

"Shhh," he says, but he's still grinning, and she notices now that he is keeping one hand behind his back.

"What do you have?" she asks.

Maybe he has made her a present. Something to remember Tembe on the day of her memorial service.

Make, Sanna thinks all of a sudden. That's it. It's what ties Hadassah's lesson of *tikkun olam* to the panels in her mom's book.

Making. Creating. And the different ways to go about that. How one person, every person, has a choice to make about how to do that.

She thinks about what Cecie has said about the branches of sadness and anger. Which one, in the end, has the best chance for helping someone make something that will actually help the world?

"You know what I was doing the past couple days," Nick says quietly, his lips almost unmoving.

"No, Nick, I don't," Sanna says.

"I was doing what you told me to do."

"I didn't tell you to do anything. I told you what I wanted to do." As she says this, she realizes she said it in the past tense. Like the way she talks about her mother now. In the past tense. Maybe it really was a branch that she went down and now she is coming back.

But it is too late for that.

Because Nick is grinning. He is clearly proud of himself. And he wants her to be, too. Her only brother. Who has also lost a mother. He is standing there in front of her, grinning, and bringing his hand out from behind his back to show her what he has made for her.

Sanna knows and does not know what it is.

"Here it is," he whispers.

"What is it?" she asks. She does not really want to know.

"It's what we need to do what we are going to do," he says.

"You brought it into the house?" she says. "What if something goes wrong? What if someone finds it?"

"We have to take that chance," he says, but she isn't sure. About anything anymore. Her rage had made things so clear to her for a while, and now that the memorial service has happened, now that the sadness is setting in, she just isn't sure again.

He is. He clearly is.

"Sanna, I thought you were going to be a warrior," he says.

"That's what you said, not me."

"You knew what I was doing."

"I didn't. How could I know?"

"I did it for you. And Tembe."

Sanna shakes her head.

"Nick," she says. "Ever since your dad was here, there's something different about you."

His eyes flash with anger. Anger is definitely the branch he's clinging to, Sanna can see that now.

"I made it for you," he says. He tries to hand it to her, but she won't reach out to take it.

"Nick, we need to think about this," she says.

"I'm done thinking. It's time for action. Here," he says, and places the device on her desk. "If you don't want to go through with your end of the plan, then don't. But I will. It's time. I can't see my mom in pain like that ever again."

"Nick, I …"

He walks toward the door and she stands in front of it, trying to block him from leaving.

"Nick, I think we may have made a mistake," she says.

"My only mistake was not doing something earlier. Who knows if Tembe would still be alive today if someone had acted earlier and given those bastards a taste of their own medicine?"

Medicine. Medicine is for healing. Sanna saw that on the night that Eden was here, helping Parker. She does not think that what Nick is doing can be called medicine.

"Think about Hadassah," Nick says, his eyes on fire. "What if someone had stopped Hitler? Don't you think she would have wanted someone to do that?"

Sanna can't speak. Her eyes are on the device on her desk. It's there now, and what happens next is up to her. That's what Nick is telling her.

He pushes her away from the door. "If you don't want to do it for your mom, then I'm going to do it for my mom." He sounds like the little boy that Sanna has seen rear up in him lately.

And then he is gone.

Part Four

1.

Almost two weeks have gone by, and each day, Parker has become happier. She cooks dinner every day again. She is not drinking as much. And she is waking early to write poems as she has always done.

But Sanna is still frozen.

Ironically, it's Parker's stability that's creating inertia in Sanna. Sanna fears saying something to Parker about Nick will upset her all over again.

As hard as it was for Parker to lose Tembe, Sanna is not sure that she could stand knowing that she might lose her son.

And so Sanna says nothing.

Sanna does not tell Parker that Nick has stopped going to school, that he drops her off every morning and picks her up every afternoon except for the one day he went into the office and changed the contact number at the school for both of them to his number, saying that their mom had died and there was a new number.

Even when he did this, Sanna stood by him and did nothing.

This is the opposite of what she imagined she would be like when she was envisioning allowing her mother's memory to lend her strength and determination. But there it is.

In all its paralytic agony.

And now, on the morning of the trip to D.C., the house is already in motion, unlike Sanna. It's long before dawn and Sanna can hear Parker having coffee with Eden and Asher at the breakfast table, talking over the rally planned for that day. They have rented an eight-passenger van and they are all going together—Parker and Nick and Sanna and Eden and Asher and Hadassah and Cecie. Seven.

There would have been room for her mom, Sanna thinks.

Would her mom have wanted to go?

What would her mom have wanted her to do?

She has fewer than twelve hours to decide. She looks at her phone. 4:22.

The ceremony is at four that afternoon. Just in time for the evening news cycle on Thanksgiving Eve.

And before that, the meeting.

The reason everyone is going is because Nick has been in contact with his father. Under the guise of wanting to reconnect and spend more time with him, Nick has convinced the senator to allow them to meet the president before the turkey pardoning. They will have five minutes. Handshakes and photos.

But it is enough, Nick has told her. It will be enough time to detonate the device.

The device still waits in the drawer of her desk in her room. She hasn't gone to any great length to hide it. Maybe she hopes Parker will find it.

She hears the doorbell ring and Hadassah and Cecie coming in. Sanna pulls the covers over her head, wanting everyone to go away.

But they won't.

She hears a knock on the door.

It's Nick.

"Squirta," he whispers as a sliver of light comes into her room like Spearfinger's knife. "Mom says you need to be getting up. We're leaving at five."

He comes into the room and shuts the door behind him, and for a moment it is blessedly dark again, but then he turns the light on.

"Hey," he says. "We need to talk before we leave."

She sits up reluctantly, sees that he is wearing a suit.

"You're wearing a suit?"

"We're going to meet the president," he says.

For a second she wonders if he has abandoned the plan, and she feels some relief, like how seeing a shore in the distance must feel for a seafarer who has been on the ocean for a long, long time.

"It's a sharp suit, if I do say so myself. And it has a lot of pockets," he says, showing her the special compartments sewn into his jacket. "That's what I wanted to talk to you about."

"Good," she says. "Sit down. I want to talk to you, too."

He sits at the desk and she thinks about the device only inches away from him.

"Nick, I've been thinking," she says. They hear laughter from the kitchen. This could be a happy day, she thinks.

"I don't think we should go through with it." There. She has said it.

"It's too late," he says coldly.

"It's never too late," she says, and feels slightly dizzy.

"Yes. Sometimes it is," he says.

"What do you mean?"

He sighs, looks at her as if she's a child. "Sanna, do you have any idea the kind of people I had to deal with in order to come this far?"

"What do you mean?"

"Do you think I did this all on my own? That I could just find some manual on the internet and do it myself? It's not as simple as that."

Sanna knows that he's been missing school. She's not sure she wants to know any more than that.

"Nick," she says. "We always have a choice." She sounds like Hadassah.

"We don't." He runs his hand through his sandy blonde hair. He looks like his father. Worried. Haggard. Determined.

"Well, you do," he says. "But I don't. That's what I wanted to talk to you about before we leave." He stops, hearing laughter from the living room.

"If you're not going to go through with it, then you need to give it back to me. Because I am going through with it. I made an agreement with some people in order to get their help. And we can't leave it here. It could be found. My mom could be implicated."

"Who gave you help? Who would find it? What are you talking about, Nick?"

"I can't tell you any more. You already know too much."

"This was my idea in the first place," she says, a bit too loudly.

"Hush," he says, and he's the big brother again. Wanting to protect her. Not thinking she can protect herself. "Listen, it's okay if you've changed your mind. But I need to know. Right now. Either you're going through with it, or you return it to me."

He waits.

She does not move.

It has become like a super power, her ability to stay still.

She could tell him she will go through with it. She can buy time that way, think about it on the four-hour drive, decide once she gets there.

That way, she can keep the decision in her own power.

This has always been about power, from the beginning.

The power to heal the hurts. The power to create justice. The power to take possession of forgotten history. The power to change the trajectory of the future.

If she tells Nick she will do it, she will be keeping all this power for herself. He thinks he is the one who has power. Because he is a boy and has made contact with other men, she is sure they must be men, who have helped him with the device. With whatever plans and deals he has made with them that will be carried out on this day.

And his father. He has made deals with his father, too. Nick has lied to him and pretended to respect him. Pretended to have forgiven, even forgotten, the past.

But it is all lies.

And Sanna, from very deep in her core, is ready for truth.

If Sanna tells Nick she is going to carry out the plan, then she will be lying, too. She will be just like him. Just like the men who lie and scheme and make deals and carry out their plans because it helps them hold the power.

Is it possible, Sanna wonders, to have truth and power at the same time?

"Sanna! Nick!" they hear Parker calling from the kitchen. "It's almost time to go. I hope you're getting ready."

"What's it going to be, Sanna?" Nick asks. "It's time to make a decision."

Sanna cannot decide. She wants this to be a dream, some kind of crazy Wizard of Oz thing that she can wake up from.

Wake. To be woke. The women in The ReSisters talk all the time about being woke. How each injustice, each outrageous thing that happens, is at the very least a way of waking those who have privilege.

As each privilege melts away, more and more people understand how the systems of power work to keep power away from everyday people.

Power. Is there any way for her have true, actual, effective power, Sanna wonders.

"Where is it, Sanna?" Nick says, his eyes glowing wilder.

"If you can't do it, fine. Fine. Whatever. But I need it."

He stands up and opens her closet door. "Where is it? Is it in here?"

He rummages around in the area above the hangers.

She has to make a choice.

She hops out of bed and goes to the desk while he's looking in the closet.

As she opens up the drawer to her desk, he hears her and turns around. He sees it in the drawer and lunges for it.

Takes it and places it into one of the pockets of his jacket.

"You can't just take it, Nick," she says. "You have to let me make a choice."

"I don't trust you, Sanna. You hesitated too long. I can't take a chance that you will change your mind. I have to take things into my own hands."

She stands there, gaping at him. She cannot believe that he's saying these things, her own brother, to her.

"Nick, you sound just like them," she says. "And what's worse, you sound like him."

His eyes flash with a hot rage, and then he snubs it out, replacing it with coldness. "Well, Sanna," he says, his voice almost a low growl like an animal would make defending its territory, "if you'd been stronger … more reliant … more determined … less like a girl, maybe this wouldn't be necessary."

"I cannot believe you actually just said that to me."

The door opens. Parker is there, smiling, excited about the trip and the people in the house.

"Oh, good, Nicky," she says. "You're dressed. And you look so nice!"

She pats his shoulder. He is taller than she is now. Then she looks at Sanna. "But, Sanna," she says, "you should have been dressed already. It's almost five, and that's when we need to leave. What's wrong with you?"

"Yeah, Sanna," Nick says slowly. "What's wrong with you?"

Parker flashes her eyes at Nick, not used to him using this tone of voice with his sister, and then decides he must be joking. She laughs and says, "Come on, now, we'll leave you to get ready and I'll pack something for you for breakfast to eat in the van. I'm so excited. It's going to be such a big day!"

She leaves and Nick moves to the door. Before leaving, he looks at Sanna one more time, pats the pocket of his jacket where he has hidden the device, and grins. She cannot believe this is the same boy she has known most of her life. She cannot believe this is someone in her family. Someone she is supposed to be able to trust.

If she tries to stop him now, if she decides to tell someone, it could affect the rest of his life.

If she doesn't, though, she thinks, and then she cannot think anymore because of the grin on his face and the words that are coming out of his mouth, like bullets, sharp and intended to harm.

"It's going to be such a big day."

2.

Sanna wishes they would be quiet. She wishes she could be alone. She needs to think. She needs to figure out how to get the device back from Nick.

But she can get neither her wishes or needs met. Not here in this van filled with talking people on the way to see the president.

"I wish we had more time with him," Cecie is saying, sitting next to Eden who is driving the van. "There are so many things I want to say to him."

"What would you say?" Eden turns to her, eyes lit up.

"I would," she pauses. "There are so many things. Black Lives Matter. Police shootings. The military-grade weapons being given to police. The drug wars that criminalize African Americans. The military that doesn't take care of veterans. The prison-industrial complex."

Eden nods. "That's a lot to cover in a five-minute photo op."

"And then there's the fact that it's all tied to the global capitalist market," says Asher from the middle row, next to Nick. "Every single one of those things you mentioned. You can see them all as arms of one beast, which is the way multinational corporations use people as capital, as cogs in the wheel of keeping wealth in the hands of the one percent."

"It's not just that," says Eden. "Racism is bound up with the rape of the earth. Our country was practically founded on it. The removal of Native Americans across the continent coincided with the discovery of silver or gold or uranium or some commodity. It's not just in history. It's happening now, too."

"You've been quiet," Cecie glances back at Hadassah in the rear-view mirror, sitting in the rear row of the van next to Sanna. "What are you thinking?"

"I'm not a morning person," says Hadassah.

The sun is not yet up, but the sky on their right is beginning to glow orange as they head north on I-95. Everyone laughs.

Sanna wonders if Hadassah can sense her desire for quiet. But then she begins to speak.

"I keep thinking about the year he was born. 1946. It was also the year that the United States officially ceased war with Germany and Japan. Before that, there were still occupied troops in both countries. Truman waited until the war crimes trials were completed."

"Can you imagine how long the war crimes trials would last if we started them now?" Nick asks.

"That's the thing," Hadassah answers. "There can be no trial when there is no official war."

"That's why The ReSisters have to work underground," says Eden from the driver's seat.

"I don't know," says Hadassah, shaking her head.

"What don't you know?" urges Nick. "Say more. Are you saying we need war?"

"I'm saying," says Hadassah, choosing her words carefully, "that I see war coming."

"It makes sense from a market perspective," Asher says.

"What kind of war?" Cecie asks. "We've got the race war, the war on drugs, the war on crime, the war on immigrants, the endless wars in Iraq and Afghanistan and Syria."

"I think," says Hadassah, "that if I could give him one message that he would really hear, it would be peace."

"Peace?" Parker says quietly from her seat by the window next to Nick. Sanna realizes she hasn't been part of the conversation until now.

"Peace," repeats Hadassah. "I foresee war."

Nick turns almost completely around in his seat. His eyes are wide. "If someone had the chance, Hadassah, before Hitler really got going, to kill him, do you think he should have?"

Asher turns his head to look at Nick.

The van finally gets quiet for longer than a minute.

"Nick," Parker says, quietly. "What a question. Of course an assassination is wrong."

"Hush, Mom," Nick snaps. "I'm talking to Hadassah."

Cecie wheels around to look at Nick and Parker, and Sanna can see the concern in her eyes at the way he spoke to Parker.

He is still waiting for Hadassah's answer.

"I have thought about that very question," Hadassah says carefully. "And I must admit that, yes, when I allow myself to feel the weight of all that happened, it might have been better. Yes."

Sanna is stunned that Nick has been given the answer he has been searching for, and from a person in the van who holds such great moral authority.

"I don't know," says Eden. "It's systemic. It's larger than one person. And it might give the ONEsters more fuel to add to their anger and violence."

"Eden could be right," says Asher.

"Hey, I know," says Nick. "Let's take a vote. It's still a democracy, right?" He's chuckling. Sanna can see that he's trying to play it off as if this is just a game to him.

"How many people would want the president killed if it would stop whatever is coming from happening?" Nick asks.

Asher raises his hand. Hadassah raises hers. Nick raises his.

Eden is keeping her hands firmly on the wheel. Cecie has her arms crossed. Sanna does not move. If Parker does not raise her hand, it could be the signal Nick needs to change his mind.

Sanna knows that no one here but she and Nick know how serious this little game is.

All eyes go toward Parker.

Please, please, Parker. Please don't raise your hand, Sanna pleads inside her head.

Parker looks at her wedding ring. Twists it slightly on her finger. "If one person could avoid going through what I have gone through," she says quietly, "it would be worth it." And as the sun breaks over the horizon in the east, she raises her hand.

3.

They stop at a gas station outside of Richmond once the sun comes up. Traffic will get worse as they get closer to D.C., and they want a chance to stretch their legs, go to the restroom, and get refills of coffee.

Sanna avoids Nick as she steps out of the van. But he follows her. She walks into the gas station and pretends to be in deep contemplation in front of the soda fountain, hoping he will leave her alone.

He doesn't.

"You heard what Hadassah said," he whispers in her ear. "You heard what Mom said. You heard it for yourself. You still think I'm doing the wrong thing?"

"Nick," she pleads.

But then someone comes in front of them and fills a big cup with ice. Something about the sound makes Sanna think twice. About her fear. About the way she runs away. She remembers back to the cold certainty she'd had when Cecie had told her that her mother was dead.

Could Nick be right?

Or is he just getting into her head?

"Say it. Say you know I'm right. Say I should do it," he says, grabbing her arm.

Sanna freezes.

"Whoa," Eden says, putting her hand on Nick's and pulling him off Sanna. "What's going on here?"

"None of your business," says Nick.

"It most certainly is," Eden says. "What are you doing grabbing your sister like that?"

Nick backs away, one step, two. Then heads to the men's room.

"Sanna," Eden says, "why was he hurting you like that?"

Sanna thinks. This is her chance. They will be in D.C. in two hours.

"Can I talk to you outside?" Sanna says to Eden, quietly, her voice cracking in the middle, surprising both Eden and herself. She didn't know she was this upset.

They walk outside and head over to a grassy area beside the gas station.

Sanna can see the traffic on 95 in the distance. It is a low hum and matches the fear she feels humming in her own blood.

"What is it?" Eden says.

"I don't know," Sanna starts.

"Sanna, you're obviously upset. What did Nick do?"

"He hasn't …."

"I can see that you're afraid. What is going on?"

Sanna can see that Eden assumes that there's some kind of abuse happening.

"It's not what you're thinking," she says.

"So tell me then."

"It's so much bigger than that."

Eden's eyes open wide.

"You can tell me anything," she says. "You can trust me."

Sanna believes her. Sanna remembers that night with Parker, how gentle Eden was with her. How Eden's whole reason for being is to bring healing. She even keeps the earth in her embrace of healing.

Sanna starts to cry.

"Sanna? Honey? What is it?"

Eden takes her into her embrace.

"Nick is going to try to kill the president," Sanna admits through tears.

"What?" Eden exclaims.

"Shh," Sanna says, looking around. She can see Asher glancing over from where he is pumping gas into the van. "I don't want anyone to know."

"That makes no sense, Sanna," Eden says. "We have to stop him."

"Please, Eden," Sanna pleads. "You said I could trust you."

Eden looks down.

"You said I could. I wouldn't have told you otherwise."

Eden looks away.

"Please don't tell anyone," Sanna says.

Eden looks back at her. "Sanna, I know I said you could trust me. But I thought it was something else then. I had no idea. How could I know?"

"But if you tell people, he will get in trouble," Sanna says.

"Are you saying you want him to go through with it?" Eden asks.

Is that what she's saying? Sanna closes her eyes and tries to think. What does she want?

She wants her mom back. She wants to wind back time. When was the last time she was happy? When was the last memory she has of being with her mom, not watching the news or talking about it with Parker in a low panic, not worried about the state of the country and the fate of the world?

Sanna tries to remember a time like this.

She can't. She honestly can't.

"Is everything okay?" Asher says. He has finished filling the gas tank for the van and has joined them.

He looks to Eden first, trying to read on her face what's happening. She is clearly upset.

And Sanna wipes tears from her cheeks, trying to wipe away the thought she was just having.

"Yes," Sanna says. "Everything is okay. I was upset about something but I'm not anymore."

Sanna looks at Eden, whose eyes are narrowed and staring at her.

"Everything is okay," Sanna says to her. "I don't know what I was talking about. It's fine."

"It's not fine," says Eden.

"What is going on?" says Asher.

Eden turns to him and Sanna can tell that she is on the verge of telling him.

"Please, Eden," Sanna begs. "You said I could trust you."

"What's going on over there?" Parker calls from the van. "It's time to get a move on!"

Eden turns back to Sanna.

"Oh, honey," she says. "You're right. If you can't trust someone, then you have nothing left. Okay. I won't say anything."

"Thank you," sighs Sanna.

"But can you promise me something?" Eden says.

"Okay."

"Let's talk about this again when we get to D.C., okay?"

"Okay."

Asher looks at both of them, holds his hands up as if saying he doesn't want to interfere any more, and walks away.

"Thank you, Eden," Sanna says once they are alone again.

"This isn't over," says Eden. "I want us to talk again when we get there. We'll have some time before the ceremony."

Sanna and Eden walk back to the van where everyone is already waiting. Sanna climbs back into the rear row as Nick stares at her from the middle seat. Eden gets back into the driver's seat and then pauses.

"Hey, Hadassah," she says, turning around. "Can you take over the driving for a while? I am suddenly feeling like I need a rest."

"I could do it," offers Cecie. Everyone knows Cecie gets car sick if she isn't in the front seat, so she either has to be in the passenger seat or driving.

"That's okay. I don't mind," says Hadassah. "I'll switch with you. It's nice and quiet back here next to Sanna. You'll get a good rest."

As they switch seats, Nick glares at Sanna.

4.

"Wanna play hangman?" Eden says, digging into her big, soft bag made of multicolored fabrics and getting out a notebook.

Sanna looks at her, not really wanting to play but needing an escape from the way Nick's turning around and staring at her as Hadassah pulls the van out of the gas station and back onto the highway.

"Sure."

Eden creates the sketch of the hangman and starts to write the lines for letters until Nick looks away.

As Sanna guesses letters and Eden writes them down, Eden also writes questions on the paper. They are yes or no questions so Sanna doesn't have to answer aloud.

"A."

Eden draws the head.

Does he have a plan? A nod for yes.

"E."

Eden writes an E at the end of the seven-letter word.

Do you know what it is? A nod again.

"I."

Eden draws the neck.

Do you think he will go through with it? Still nodding.

"M."

Eden draws the body.

Do you want to stop him? Sanna stops nodding. But doesn't shake her head for no.

"F."

Eden draws the right arm.

Do you know what you want to do? Sanna shakes her head.

"S."

Eden draws the left arm.

Can I talk to Asher about this? Slowly, Sanna nods.

"T."

Eden writes a T as the first letter of the world.

"P."

Eden draws the left leg. One limb to go.

"O."

Eden writes an O in the third space.

Sanna looks at the word. T __ O __ __ __ E

It looks like "toe," and Sanna thinks of words it could be but not quite.

Topple. Torture.

"N."

"Hangman," says Eden, and draws the right leg. Then she fills in the rest of the letters to create the word.

Trouble.

Sanna looks away as Eden gets out her phone and texts Asher.

"Sanna and I need to talk to you. Alone."

Sanna watches as he gets the alert, looks at the text and nods without looking back at them.

He sees a sign for Pocahontas State Park and says to the group, "Hey, can we stop there for a little bit? We're making pretty good time."

Sanna chimes in and says, "Good idea. I think my mom would like that."

And Hadassah takes the next exit off the highway.

5.

The park is open but deserted at this time of the morning. Theirs is the only car in the parking lot, yet Parker reaches into her wallet to get a five-dollar bill for the entrance fee.

"Honor system," she says as she stuffs the money into the little metal box. "The irony of that."

They start to walk down the self-guided interpretative trail, stopping to read the signs about the people who used to live here.

"They always write Native American history in the third-person and past tense," says Hadassah. "As if there is no one left to tell their own stories."

Sanna spots a huge, ancient oak tree, still filled with colored leaves even this late in the season, and says, "I'm going to go take some photos over there."

She's hoping Eden and Asher follow her, and they do.

She snaps a few photos, making her way around the gigantic trunk to an area that is blocked from the view of those still on the path.

"What's up?" says Asher, looking back and forth at Sanna and Eden, waiting for someone to say something.

"Sanna has some information," Eden says. "We thought you should know."

"Information?" he asks. "What is it?" He looks directly at Sanna, cocks his head slightly.

This moment could be her *tikkun olam*, she thinks. In this moment, she has a choice. But she cannot decide whether telling him will lead to the outcome she wants.

"Asher," she says, "I have something to tell you because I need your help. But before I do, I need you to know that I must be in control."

He narrows his eyes at her.

"I know you understand about freedom and agency," she continues. "I know you get that. So what you need to know is that this was my idea, and somehow it's gotten out of control. And I want control back."

"Just tell him," says Eden. "We don't have much time."

Sanna takes a deep breath and dives in. "After my mom was imprisoned, I started thinking about ways I could help. I went to my mom's friends for advice. Nothing seemed very effective. I felt helpless."

He nods.

"And then she was killed. And my desire to help turned to an ice-cold rage."

He stands very still. Eden looks to make sure no one's nearby.

"I decided I wanted to kill the president," she says.

His eyes widen but he says nothing.

"I told Nick. It was right after his dad showed up. He joined in the plan. But it got out of hand."

"How do you mean?" Asher asks quietly.

"He … I'm not sure exactly. But he hasn't been going to school. I think he's involved with some very bad dudes. I feel like something's going to happen that wasn't what I intended."

He waits. Nods. Encouraging her to go on.

"He has a device that he's going to take into our meeting at the White House."

"But we'll be searched," he says.

"He's going to meet his dad at another entrance. He's been in contact with him, buttering him up to make this work so he can get in without security."

"We've got to stop him," says Eden. "This isn't what The ReSisters are about."

"The poll Nick took earlier in the van?" Asher asks. "This is what that was about?"

Sanna nods. "And the score was four to three."

"I voted for it," says Asher, running his hands through his hair. "Okay, let me think." He looks up through the branches of the old oak tree.

"Are you sure you don't want him to go through with it?" he asks.

"Asher," Eden chides.

Sanna nods. "Remember what I said about control? This whole thing started because it was my mom who was killed. Mine. Hadassah let me read a book my mom created before she died. I wanted to do something that would make my mom proud. Mine. Mine, do you get it?"

Asher watches her and nods slowly.

"It was my idea. I wanted to do it. But I don't anymore. And Nick has become a bully, just like his dad, just like the president. He has taken control away from me. And I want it back. Can you see that?"

Asher nods.

"I think I can help him understand," he says slowly. "You've got to get it back."

6.

"Well, that was depressing," says Parker, back in the van, as they pull out of the parking lot.

"It was a nice park," says Cecie. "But just putting up a few historical markers doesn't seem like doing the most."

Hadassah takes off her coat as the heat comes on and says, "It's always been interesting to me how little America remembers its history compared to other countries that have had trauma. It's like a badge of honor in Germany to remember."

"It took forever just to put a little sign and a bench up on Sullivan's Island off the South Carolina coast," Cecie says. "Do you remember that? To mark the place where millions of slaves entered the country. They called it the black Ellis Island. And put up a bench."

"Tembe always said there was so much more that we could do to enlist artists to help us remember," Parker says quietly and looks out the window.

"I've been thinking about the mass shootings," Asher says, and everyone turns to look at him.

"What does that have to do with anything?" Nick asks. Sanna can see he's disturbed.

"So many of them were done by men who had a history of domestic violence against their wives and children."

Sanna is not sure where he is going with this.

Cecie laughs, but it's a cold laugh. "Oh, I get it," she says. "You're saying what if we put a historical marker on every house where violence has occurred? How many houses wouldn't have one?"

"Something like that," Asher says. Nick's still staring at him.

"It happened to me," Parker says quietly, and Nick's head swivels from Asher to her.

"Mom," he pleads. "Don't."

"Why not, Nick? These are our best friends in the whole world. Hadassah was Tembe's best friend. Eden and Asher came over to help me on the darkest day of my life. Cecie was there when your dad showed up. She saw what he was like. Why shouldn't I be able to talk to them about anything?"

"Tell us, Parker." Sanna says the words before she can stop herself. She is tired of seeing men telling women not to speak, tired of men in power silencing women, and most of all, tired of the man Nick seems to be becoming.

"Nick's father was violent," Parker says. "To me and to him. It started when Nick was a baby."

"Mom," Nick says.

"It was awful. I wanted to leave but I was afraid. I didn't know where to go. I thought he would follow me. I lived in constant fear. No, that's not true. The thing is, there were very good times. He could be so tender and understanding. Sweet, really. It was a cycle. I was trapped. I don't know what would have happened if I hadn't met Tembe."

"What did my mom have to do with it?" Sanna asks.

"Your mom saw what no one else could see. How I needed help. To get out."

"You mean you started dating Tembe when you were still married to my dad?" Nick sneers.

"Jesus, Nick," cries Asher. "What makes you such a moral authority all of a sudden? Your mom's telling us how Tembe saved her life."

"I just didn't ever know that," Nick says, sinking back into his seat.

"How did my mom help you exactly?" Sanna asks. It's like her whole being has turned into a dry carcass and Parker has the words she needs to be alive again.

Parker turns and extends her hand into the last row of the van, reaching for Sanna.

"She loved me," Parker says with tears in her eyes. "She loved me so very deeply that I realized I had to leave him because I deserved better. She taught me that violence only leads to more violence, and that love is the answer."

Sanna thinks for a beat, and then something occurs to her. "How did she know that about violence?"

Parker blinks. Wipes away a tear. Hesitating, Sanna can tell.

"Because of your father. The reason you never knew him? He was violent, too."

"What is this?" quips Nick. "The Nurenburg Van?"

But no one laughs.

"What do you mean, Parker?" Sanna says quietly.

"Your mom was dating him. And then decided she didn't want to anymore. But he wouldn't let her go." Parker is looking down at her wedding rings on the hand that is holding Sanna's. It's almost as if they are praying together, Sanna thinks.

"And?" she asks.

"He raped her," Parker says quietly. "She got pregnant."

"And made me?" Sanna asks. Some part of her has always known this. Some part of her recognized that the strength and ferocity of her mother must have come from a very deep hurt.

"Yes," Parker almost whispers. "When she found out she was pregnant, that's when she moved to Pennsylvania. That's when we met."

"But I would have been only two then," Nick says.

"Yes, Nick. I knew Tembe for five years before I could find the courage to leave your father."

Nick shifts into a sulky silence.

Sanna squeezes Parker's hand. "I'm sorry for what happened to you and Nick," she says. "And thank you for telling me about what happened to my mom."

There is a strength in her that she is feeling now that she has never felt. But then something hits her.

"Wait. My dad. Where is he?"

"Died in a car crash when you were a baby. Your grandmother called to tell your mom, and that's why your mom felt safe enough to take you to Cherokee for visits."

Both of my parents are dead, Sanna thinks, but she doesn't say it out loud for fear of hurting Parker.

"I love you, Parker," she says instead and lets go of Parker's hand after giving it a squeeze. Then she taps on Nick's shoulder. "Hey, brother, when we get to D.C., I need to talk to you. Alone."

7.

Hadassah gets on 395 heading into D.C. at a little before ten in the morning. They have made good time, even with their two stops, and the view of the Lincoln Memorial as they cross Arlington Memorial Bridge is stunning.

"Can we stop there?" Sanna asks from the rear of the van. "I've always wanted to see that."

"Sure, honey," says Hadassah. No one has said much since Parker's revelation, and certainly no one wants to say no to Sanna now.

After they park, Sanna grabs Nick's hand and walks quickly toward the monument, gaining a distance between them and the others.

"What's going on, Sanna? You're acting weird," he says.

She says nothing, just keeps walking. Pulling him along like a recalcitrant child.

When they arrive at the steps and look up at the huge seated Lincoln, she says, "Give it to me."

"What?"

"Give it to me," she repeats. "It was my idea. I should be the one to do it."

"You won't be able to get through security. Only my dad—"

"Bullshit," she snaps. "And you know it. If you want to get me through security, you can."

"But I want—"

"You know what, Nick? I don't really care what you want. This was my idea and you stole it from me. It was my mom who was imprisoned. Not yours. My mom who was killed. Not yours. And I am sick and tired of men like this president and your dad and ...," she takes a deep breath and then says it, "And like my dad—and like *you*—doing whatever they want. It's time for women to do what we want. And I want you to give it to me. It's my decision to make, Nick. Not yours."

He stands with his mouth open and eyes wide but says nothing. Then, very slowly, he walks to the statue of Lincoln and goes around to the left side of the steps.

She follows him.

"Martin Luther King, Junior gave his 'I Have a Dream' speech from the eighteenth step, right up there. Did you know that?" he says, and, almost imperceptibly, he places the device in her hand. She quickly tucks it into a zippered compartment of her purse.

"You'll have to be nice to my dad," he says. "You'll have to convince him that you're excited to be there and that you like the president."

She nods.

"It's set to detonate at one p.m.," he says. "Just at the time of our meeting. You have to keep it safe until then."

"I can do that," she says and shoots one last glance up at Lincoln as they walk away.

8.

Sanna feels how the power has shifted back to her after getting the device. As they tumble back into the van for the final leg of the journey, she pats the purse sitting in her lap and thinks back to the circles in her mother's book as she feels her body making the circles through D.C.'s many roundabouts.

"There's a very good Indian restaurant two blocks from the White House," Hadassah says as they get close. "Shall we have lunch there before we go? I think they have a buffet, so it shouldn't take too long."

There are murmurs of agreement and Hadassah pulls the van into a parking garage off K Street. They circle up three flights before finding a space. The third panel in her mother's book was about justice. What is true and right. Honest and outright. Sanna takes this as the sign she needs to do what she must do.

As they head down the stairs in the parking garage—more circles— Sanna decides she's going to use their time at lunch to tell a story. She wants someone to know how she's feeling, and, while she can't reveal to them what is going to happen, she hopes one of them will remember what she says at the lunch.

They place their coats on chairs at a large round table and head to the buffet line. Sanna keeps her purse on her shoulder. It bumps reassuringly against her hip as she fills her plate with naan and pakora and vegetable biryani and an unusual kale and spinach kofta.

Dipping her naan into the tamarind sauce once they are back at the table, she asks, "Does anyone know the story of Spearfinger?"

"I remember your mom mentioning it, but not the details," says Parker, spearing a piece of tandoori paneer.

"It's an old Cherokee legend," Sanna explains. "It's been on my mind today for some reason."

"What is it?" Cecie asks, and Sanna has the invitation she needs to dive in.

"As the weather turned cold," she says, "the Cherokee people in the mountains would sometimes hear a voice in the night. Some people said it was the wind whipping through the trees as the leaves emptied their branches, but other people said it was a woman."

"There's a story like that in Mexican-American culture," says Cecie. "She's called La Llorona, and wails in the night, tempting children to come to her."

"I didn't know that," says Sanna. "That's what happens with Spearfinger, too. She tricks children into coming near her."

"I've often wondered why the scariest stories in many cultures have to do with women," says Hadassah. "Lilith, who was Adam's first wife, is often depicted as a witch."

"The poet Anne Sexton wrote a book of poems called *Transformations* to try to come to terms with these witch stories from the Grimm Brothers," adds Parker.

Sanna nods. She knows Sexton is one of Parker's favorite poets, and she says, "Transformations is a great word for what Spearfinger does. Because at first she seems like a kind old granny, and that's how she traps the children."

"Like in Hansel and Gretel," says Eden.

"Wow, there really are a lot of scary old women stories," muses Asher.

"It's a lot like Hansel and Gretel," continues Sanna, "but instead of a little cottage, her whole body becomes stone, like the stone boulders that make up the mountains."

"So she's actually the land itself?" Eden asks.

"Maybe," says Sanna. "But that's not the worst part."

"Why are you telling us this?" Nick asks, but she ignores his question.

"Let me guess," says Asher, fully absorbed by the story. "It has to do with her finger, right? As a spear? A phallic symbol?"

Sanna nods and holds up her knife. "Exactly. When the children get close enough, she uses her long pointer finger like a spear and stabs them, scooping out their livers and eating them."

There are cries of disgust all around the table. "What a story to tell over lunch!" says Nick.

But Sanna likes telling the story. She enjoys using her voice in this way, captivating her audience and holding their attention in her hands with her words.

"That's not the end, though," Sanna says. "There's more to the story."

They stare at her.

"One day, the people decide they want to kill Spearfinger."

"Interesting," says Cecie. "This isn't part of the La Llorona story."

"Well," says Sanna, "the people lured Spearfinger to their village with a great fire because they knew she was attracted to smoke. When she got close, they threw their spears at her, but the spears did not hurt her because her skin was stone."

"You cannot use a material to destroy the same material," says Hadassah. "Do you remember Audre Lorde saying 'The master's tools will never dismantle the master's house'?" she asks, and Parker and Cecie nod.

"Tembe believed that," says Hadassah. "It's why she thought that art was the way to bring about peace."

"What happens next, Sanna?" Parker asks, clearly drawn in by the story.

"Well, two birds come."

"Of course," smiles Eden.

"One is Titmouse, and he begins to sing the word 'Heart, heart.' The villagers think he's telling them to aim for her heart. So they do. But again, the arrowheads shatter and fall to the ground. The people are mad at Titmouse and kill him for lying."

"I'm remembering this now," Parker says slowly. "Who was the other bird?"

"Chickadee."

"Of course!" Parker grins. "That's your mom's nickname for you!"

Sanna nods, very serious, and continues. "Chickadee was a very brave bird. She knew what Titmouse was trying to tell the people, but he hadn't done it correctly."

She looks directly at Nick when she says this.

"So Chickadee musters up her courage and flies toward Spearfinger. Lands on her long finger with the spear. Because the hand is where her heart resides."

"*Tikkun olam*," says Hadassah quietly.

"They immediately understand what Chickadee is telling them, and they aim for the hand, where Chickadee is perched, killing Spearfinger."

"What happens to Chickadee?" Cecie asks, eyes wide.

"She is killed, too," says Sanna. "But ever after, she is remembered as Truth Teller, and when we see her chickadee bird relatives, we know that a loved one who is away on a journey will return safely home."

"Fascinating," says Eden. "I have had chickadees who landed on my hands when I sat very still in the arboretum."

"Well, Chickadee," Parker says to Sanna, using the nickname that they will all now remember, "thank you for your wonderful storytelling. It's now time to go see Spearfinger in the White House."

Several of them laugh.

Sanna does not.

9.

They walk the two blocks south back through Lafayette Park together, and then at Pennsylvania Avenue, they pause, Nick and Sanna preparing to veer right toward the Executive Office Building while the others go left toward the Visitors' Entrance.

"How will we meet up with you, though?" Parker asks. "I don't understand why we can't come with you."

"I told you," Nick says. "My dad has arranged a special pass for the two of us, but not for everyone."

Sanna sees Asher and Eden glance at each other warily.

"We've got to go," Nick says, looking at his phone to check the time. "We'll come get you in the Visitors Foyer once you get through security."

He grabs Sanna's hand and walks away.

Sanna feels her heart beating to the tips of her right hand fingers as she clutches her purse at her side. Like Spearfinger. But like Chickadee, too. Because she checked on her phone in the car after the Lincoln Memorial and discovered that bags of any kind are not allowed in the White House.

"I'm here to see Senator Jones," says Nick to the security guard at the entrance to the EOB. "I'm his son. This is my sister."

The security guard picks up a phone—an actual phone with a cord, Sanna notices—and dials a number.

"One of his aides will be right down to get you," the security guard says. "You can sit over there."

They perch on a bench in the hallway.

The guard didn't say anything about her bag.

Sanna has no time to think, for soon a young woman is smiling and waving them through past the security guard's desk and they're taking an elevator up to the third floor where the White House Staff has offices.

Nick smirks at her in the elevator and she looks away.

As the elevator doors open, there is a large red digital clock on the wall that says 12:41.

"Son!"

The senator is standing under the clock, grinning wildly and then pumping Nick's hand, slapping him on the back, completely ignoring Sanna, who stands there knowing she has nineteen—no, now eighteen minutes—to go.

"Let's go meet the president, shall we?" Senator Jones says, pointing down a hallway.

"What about the rest of us?" Sanna asks.

Senator Jones stops grinning and says, "Who are you?"

"This is Sanna," Nick says. "My sister."

The senator's eyebrows go up. "My stepsister," Nick corrects himself. "Don't you remember her from when you came to the house?"

The senator waves his hand as if erasing the memory. "What 'rest of us' does she mean?" he asks Nick.

"The group we came with. Nick's mom. My mom's best friends," she says.

Sixteen minutes.

"This was just for you, son," the senator says. "A special gift from your father. I thought you knew that."

"I—I—" Nick stammers.

"Nick!" Sanna says. "We—." But then she stops. What is she saying? Wouldn't it be best for the others not to be there after all? She thought by now they would have asked her to leave the purse somewhere. She had not envisioned this.

"We can't leave the president waiting," the senator says and starts walking down the hall.

Nick follows him.

All of a sudden, she hears the voice.

10.

The voice they made fun of during the election, Tembe and Parker, while watching the news. The voice they mocked together as a buffoon, and then later, after he rose to power, cursed together, as decision after decision cut funding for the arts, took rights from citizens, rounded up immigrants, emboldened the police, protected gun owners, slashed education, instituted the One Nation Education Policy, and threatened their family with annihilation in everything from wedding cakes to her mother's actual death.

She envisions doing it.

She can hear his voice, booming and bullying, even in everyday conversation. She can just walk down this hallway with Nick and his dad. She can walk into the office. She can even shake his hand and say "Nice to meet you."

She imagines his hand, clammy and soft, even while wielding such power. The hand of a man who at heart is actually a coward. The bullying comes from such a deep place of fear and feeling unloved that he must lash out to protect his secret weakness.

She sees herself placing the purse on the desk as they gather for a picture. The president behind the desk. And the senator near him, putting his arm around Nick. She would pause and ask if she could take a photo of the three of them with her phone, and they would smile. Proud of themselves. Three men. Their grins and suits and white teeth showing their power.

Leaving the purse on the desk, she would step back to get them all in the photo.

She would glance at the time in the upper right of her phone's screen. One minute to go.

"Hold on," she would say. "I have a new app I want to use. It takes fabulous photos. Let me open it."

And the president would laugh and say, "Yes, go ahead. Because I should look as good as I can."

And the senator would laugh, the sycophant, murmuring some compliment, and as the words slip from his tongue, the device would go off, and while Nick would be hurt, he knew that he would when he worked with whomever helped him to make the device, he got dressed this morning in that coat and that tie knowing that this is how it would end, and the vision that Sanna had on the night of her mother's death would finally come to fruition.

Nick wanted this to happen.

Hadassah said she would have stopped Hitler.

Parker raised her hand, too.

Even Asher and Eden, who knew what might happen, did not stop them when they parted on Pennsylvania Avenue. Maybe they thought there would still be time. Maybe they figured Sanna would dispose of the device before it came to this.

Sanna stops.

Looks down at the rug beneath her feet.

There is a white circle on the blue rug that holds the presidential seal.

The circle in her mother's book.

The very first panel.

And the words: "You can't make it."

"I can't."

The words are out of her mouth and Nick and the senator are turning around to face her but she is already gone.

11.

She opens the door to the nearby stairwell and runs down the steps as fast as she can.

Tracing the circles she has traveled, not just today, at the traffic intersections and in the parking garage, but in her mind. Her whole life is coming full circle as she grasps the hand rail, hoping she will not fall, hoping her feet will allow her to make it down the three flights and out the door in time.

The third panel of her mother's book comes to her. Fighting is a way of moving your feet.

This is what Sanna sees herself as doing. Fighting like the Cherokee have always fought. In the Ring Fight. In the Trail of Tears. In every pow wow dance.

Using their feet to make a change that claims power in a different way.

The good, red way.

This is exactly what her mother would want her to do, Sanna is sure now, as she bursts from the stairwell back onto the main floor and runs toward the door.

"Miss!" the security guard calls to her.

She is at the door. Her hand is on the large metal doorknob.

Her hand.

Like Spearfinger's.

With the power to destroy.

She turns the knob and feels the cold air from the late November afternoon rush at her, takes one step out, and then there is a hand on her shoulder.

"Miss?" she hears a man saying from behind. "Is something wrong?"

"Please don't," she begs, her eyes scanning the hallway behind him as she sees two Secret Service agents running toward her.

"Don't what, miss?" the security guard asks.

"Don't stop me," she says.

Her eyes go up to the red glowing clock above the security guard's desk.

12:59.

She takes one hand. The hand that has worn the glove of Spearfinger. The hand that held her mother's as they crossed the street together when she was younger. And she dives that hand into her purse, reaching for the device, hoping to toss it away in time, not wanting to hurt anyone.

She thinks of the fourth panel of her mother's book. Hurt and injury happen when truth and transparency are washed away.

"It's a bomb," she is whispering to the security guard, hoping that revealing this truth will save him and anyone else from being hurt. "I'm trying to get rid of it. Like Chickadee."

She reaches her hand up and sees the confusion in his eyes as he stares at the device in her hand.

She cocks her arm back and turns away from the building.

Nick always did say she threw like a girl.

Maybe today, that will be a good thing.

As the device is released from her hand and goes flying toward the lawn, a shot rings out.

She hears and does not hear, like her mother before her, the explosion as it detonates thirty yards from the building.

She feels and does not feel, unlike her mother before her, the warmth of her own blood seeping across the area of her chest as the secret security agent's bullet lodges in her heart.

No one else got hurt.

She did not use the master's tools, she imagines herself saying to Hadassah one day, petting Winston the cat in her back yard.

Maybe it will be spring.

Maybe someone else will be the president.

Maybe her mother's book will be understood by someone who has the power to make a difference.

Because no one is hurt.

Except Chickadee.

12.

She sees both cars in the driveway and smiles as she tells the cab driver that this is it. Her home. Everything looks the same except that the red leaves that were just turning on the dogwood tree in the front yard are now all completely gone.

It is Thanksgiving Day. She imagines the look on their faces when she surprises them. She can almost smell the turkey roasting in the oven as she takes out her keys and unlocks the front door.

The plan came to her as she came out of the coma a few days before.

"Is there anyone you want me to call?" asked the nurse.

She shook her head. "Let me surprise them," she said to the nurse.

And this is it.

The moment she has been waiting for.

The left side of her face and neck are still bandaged from the burns. Underneath the white cotton, her skin is tight and mottled like stone. It itches. She stops herself from scratching it.

"Hello?" she calls into the house. "Guess who's home?"

No answer.

She goes to the kitchen. The oven is off. No turkey inside. No pots of gravy or mashed potatoes on top of the stove.

She looks in the refrigerator. The turkey sits, cold and still wrapped in plastic, on the bottom shelf.

Six mugs with dregs of coffee still in them sit on the counter. Why so many, she wonders, and heads to the bedrooms.

The first one she enters is Sanna's. The bed is made. She smiles. Sits on the bed. Picks up a pillow and smells it. It lingers with Sanna's sweet scent.

Where can she be?

She walks down the hall and goes into her room.

Everything is as she left it. Parker's boots by the closet. A photo of them by the bed.

Her heart beats in an erratic rhythm.

Something is wrong.

This is not how she imagined it. Any of it. Her homecoming. Her return. Thanksgiving Day.

She sits down on the bed and looks at her hands.

She hears the metallic click of a chickadee and looks up toward the window.

"Chickadee," she says out loud toward the bird. "Where are you?"

And later, after she discovers what has happened, Tembe will never be able to look at her own hands without seeing the skin like stone and the index finger with a sharp spear at the end.

ᎤᏓᏛᏗ

is
pronounced
doyugodv

and means
justice
and
truth
and
right
and
honest
and
outright
and
English
has so many words
for something
that sounds like
"Do you, duh?"

O'HCA SHIA

Hurt and injury happen when the circle is broken and truth justice honesty and outright transparency are washed away.

DWᎥ alasdi or fight is not the same word we think of as fighting and is connected to the words for baseball football dancing economics and trampling. It means to use your feet.

Body also
means
health
and is connected
to the words
for
nation
capital
taxes
funds
anarchy
and
diameter.
It
is all
a
circle.

DβM

 OᎤWOᎡA

God
unelanvhi
and
fun
uwotlvdi
become
nature
unelanvuwotlv
and God
unelanvhi
and
guard
agatiya
(also connected to
wait
agatisdia)
become
providence
unelanvhiagatiya.

About the Author and Artist

Cassie Premo Steele holds a Ph.D. in Comparative Literature and Women's, Gender and Sexuality Studies from Emory University in Atlanta. She is the author of 15 books, including most recently *Tongues in Trees: Poems 1994-2017*, and her poetry has been nominated six times for the Pushcart Prize. Her nonfiction books include *We Heal from Memory: Sexton, Lorde, Anzaldúa and The Poetry of Witness* and *Earth Joy Writing: Creating Harmony through Journaling and Nature.* Her first novel, *Shamrock and Lotus*, is available from All Things That Matter Press. She lives with her wife and daughter in Columbia, South Carolina.

Amy Alley is an artist, writer, educator, knitter, happy mother of a teenager, and all-around creative being who strives to bring her love of nature and echoes of her Native heritage to all her work. Her art is in public and private collections nationally and abroad. Her first novel, *The Absence of Anyone Else,* was published in 2010 and will be available as a second edition print with book club questions in Fall of 2018. She maintains a blog at www.panpanstudios.blogspot.com. She enjoys reading, snail mail, black coffee, sweater weather, and visiting Finland, home of her heart. She lives with her son in Upstate South Carolina.

ALL THINGS THAT MATTER PRESS

FOR MORE INFORMATION ON TITLES AVAILABLE FROM
ALL THINGS THAT MATTER PRESS, GO TO
http://allthingsthatmatterpress.com
or contact us at
allthingsthatmatterpress@gmail.com

Made in the USA
Columbia, SC
28 September 2018